*Two rebellious cousins—and
the men who tame them!*

Meet Caitlin and Maddie: two beautiful,
spirited cousins seeking to overcome family
secrets and betrayal....

Neither cousin is looking for marriage—these Texas
women have proud, rebellious hearts and it will
take two very powerful men to tame them.

But look out, Caitlin and Maddie—two tough,
gorgeous guys are about to try and sweep you up
the aisle...and they won't take no for an answer!

These two rebel brides are about to
meet their match at last.
This month, enjoy Caitlin's story in
To Claim a Wife

Next month, meet Maddie in
To Tame a Bride (#3560)

Dear Reader,

I've dedicated the two books in this series, REBEL BRIDES, to my mother. My first heroine, Caitlin, lost her mother at an early age; and my second heroine, Maddie, was abandoned by her mother. But I'd like you all to know that my mother is the best mother a kid could have.

She and I are not only mother and daughter, but best friends. I am so blessed to have been raised by such a gentle, compassionate, loving woman, and her unconditional love for me is truly the most profound gift a mother could give her child. My mom's love of cowboys, the American West and country music turned out to be genetic. And, of course, my mom is my number-one fan. But then, she'd be that even if I'd never written a single book.

Thank you so much for reading my books. I've had the time of my life writing them for you. I hope you read something in them that you find encouraging and uplifting.

May your life be filled with happily-ever-afters!

Becca Fox

To Claim a Wife
Susan Fox

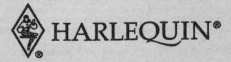

TORONTO • NEW YORK • LONDON
AMSTERDAM • PARIS • SYDNEY • HAMBURG
STOCKHOLM • ATHENS • TOKYO • MILAN • MADRID
PRAGUE • WARSAW • BUDAPEST • AUCKLAND

For my mother, Marvel Terry. The sweetest, most loving
mother on planet Earth, and the gentlest, classiest, most
honorable woman I know. I love you with all my heart. I
can't find adequate words to express how much you
mean to me. God bless you.

ISBN 0-373-03556-X

TO CLAIM A WIFE

First North American Publication 1999.

Copyright © 1999 by Susan Fox.

CHAPTER ONE

THE letter was as terse as a telegram.

> Return to the Broken B. Jess Bodine dying.
> Coulter City Hospital ICU.
>
> RD

Caitlin Bodine wasn't shocked by the news of her father's grave illness. She'd known he was dying. News had a way of reaching her. It wasn't that she still had many friends in Coulter City, Texas, but a man as important in ranching and oil as Jess Bodine was news anywhere in ranch country. Even in ranch country as remote as the plains of eastern Montana.

Caitlin had agonized for months over the news of her father's worsening health. Agonized, wrote letters, then suffered his inevitable silence when her efforts to mend the breach between them failed as abysmally as always.

But then, her father had never acknowledged any of her other letters. Five years of utter silence from him should have been enough to convince her that their estrangement would continue to the grave. But that tiny spark of hope—the one she'd carried since she was a small child—refused to die.

It was a fact that she'd always idolized her father. It was also a fact that her father had rejected her. Her childhood craving to be accepted and loved by him still had the power to torment her, still had the power to seduce her back to Texas for one last colossal heartbreak.

Perhaps this time things would be different. Perhaps in the face of death, the old man's thoughts about his only child had become remorseful. Perhaps he'd come to regret exiling her five years before.

But the bitter reality was that it wasn't her father who'd summoned her home, it was Reno Duvall. Reno Duvall, the man who hated her.

Strangely, she dreaded facing Reno's hatred even more than she dreaded another rejection from her father. Old memories stirred forcefully and panic sent a poison arrow through her insides.

Reno would never forgive her. But then, Caitlin might never forgive herself.

Reno Duvall walked down the hospital corridor to the ICU. He remembered Caitlin Bodine as an eighteen-year-old hellion, who'd dogged her father's footsteps and engaged in a near cutthroat competition with his younger brother, Beau, for her father's attention. She'd been a solemn, moody adolescent who hid her pain behind temper tantrums and frequent retreats to her secret place on the range.

She'd been a child perpetually frustrated and injured by her failure to live up to her father's expectations, a child so pathologically jealous of his younger brother that she'd come to hate the stepbrother—the *rival*—who'd become her nemesis instead of the rightful member of her family that her father's marriage had made him.

Had her jealousy of Beau been so bitter, so deep that she truly had caused Beau's death, then allowed him to die? Witnesses had testified at the inquest that she'd done everything she could to save him.

But she'd failed. She'd been the one to put Beau's life in danger in the first place, running off in another wild temper to hide out on the range. She'd known about the flash flood warnings in the area, but she'd ignored the danger.

Reno hardened his heart to the emotionally neglected child she'd been. Whatever had caused her tantrum that day, her selfish actions had set the stage for Beau's death. Eighteen was too damned young to die.

Though Reno had sent for her to come home to the Broken B, he'd loathed the chore. Loathed the notion of ever coming face-to-face with the girl—the woman—who'd destroyed his family. His mother was gone now too, because of Caitlin. Her grief over her youngest son's death had been as intense on the day she'd died as it had been the day they'd carried Beau's slicker-shrouded body into the ranch yard.

A man couldn't overlook that. Or the grim fact that Caitlin Bodine was kin to him, though there was no blood between them. No blood, that is, except his kid brother's lifeblood.

Reno was about to enter the ICU when the elevator down the hall arrived. He sensed—he *knew*—the moment the doors slid open who would step out.

The past five years hadn't changed Caitlin Bodine, yet the five years between then and now had changed everything about her.

She seemed taller now, prouder, almost arrogant. Her slender body moved with the poise and elegance of a model, but with a kind of confidence he somehow sensed was pure playacting. The coltishness of her slim figure was gone; she'd acquired a womanly roundness that sent a tremor of restlessness to his groin.

He made himself focus on her face. She'd lost the adolescent fullness in her cheeks. Her cheekbones seemed higher, her features sharper, more strikingly patrician. Her lips were the same, lush and naturally dark.

She wore her sable hair long and loose. It was longer now, rippling down her shoulders and back until it swung past her tight little backside like the thick flowing mane of a show horse. Long hair had always drawn him, but the sight had never hit him like this, never heated his blood in quite this way or sent it pumping through him like a hot pulse. It was just one more reason to nurse the hatred he felt for her.

But when those incredible jewel-blue eyes, with their thick fringe of black feathery lashes, shifted and homed in on him, he suddenly saw the girl again. The child. The broken-hearted, angry, hungry-for-love child she'd been every day that he'd known her. Something moved in his heart, but he ruthlessly ignored it.

The moment she stepped off the elevator, Caitlin sensed Reno's presence. Terror sent talons of actual pain through her, but before she lost her nerve—or showed a glimmer of weakness—she made herself look straight at him.

Five years had made Reno harder and more formidable than ever. She'd secretly loved him once, adored him. She'd hated his brother for his little cruelties and for the way her father had blatantly favored him. But she'd loved Reno Duvall. Loved him, fantasized about him, and cried into her pillow at night because he was just like her father: stern, remote, unattainable.

He was so big. His shoulders were so wide, his body leanly muscled and as hard as a work saddle. Beneath his overlong black hair, his rugged, weather-tanned features were handsome in the rough handsome way of Western men in their prime. But so hard. And unforgiving. Relentlessly unforgiving.

She recognized the harsh lights in his eyes and knew that he'd never changed his mind about her, that he'd never believed her innocence, never forgiven her. After all this time, he probably never would.

The hurt she felt wasn't unexpected, but it threatened the poised facade she'd worked so hard for. Somehow, she dug deeper for the strength that heartache and banishment had forged in her.

She continued in Reno's direction without faltering. She got within speaking distance, then asked, "Is he still alive?"

She knew the question sounded cold. She'd meant for it to. She would exchange no pleasantries with Reno Duvall. He'd slice her to bits verbally if she did.

Something flared in Reno's eyes and they burned over her face. His voice was harsh.

"Said he'd see you when you got here."

Reno eased aside and Caitlin walked past him. He turned and walked a half pace behind her as they entered the ICU.

The patient cubicles faced the nurses' station in a semicircle. Caitlin looked through the glass walls into each one as they passed, until they came to the fourth. Reno made a brief gesture—she was aware of every move he made—and she stopped. Foreboding quaked through her as she stared past the glass.

At first she didn't recognize the elderly man on the hospital bed. Jess Bodine's hair had gone from iron gray to nearly white. An oxygen tube ran across his craggy face.

As Caitlin stepped into the cubicle, the blip of monitors made an impression and she took swift note of the array of machines that flanked the head of the bed. Though they'd walked in quietly, the old man heard and gave a restless move of his head before he opened his eyes.

Jess Bodine had been almost as tall as Reno, built as strongly and as hard. But the old man on the bed seemed smaller. He looked frail, his face deathly pale and more gaunt than lean. Even his brown eyes—when she got close enough to see—seemed faded.

The shock of discovering that her rugged, larger-than-life father was now a thin, broken-looking old man, sent a spear of anguish through her heart.

She was truly losing him. The reminder made a more painful impact on her than it had when she'd heard he was ill. Jess was so near death that it was clear to her that there was no time left to bridge the emotional chasm between them. She might never learn what it was about her that he'd found so unlovable.

Though Jess Bodine was pitifully wasted and weak, his eyes fixed on her and gleamed with recognition. A moment later, he spoke. The words of welcome and forgiveness she'd hungered to hear never came.

"You see she gets the blood test."

The incredible demand was made of Reno. The shock wave of silence that followed made her ill. Her soft "Hello, Daddy," was little more than a whisper.

Jess's gaze flickered briefly, then dulled. "We'll see whether you got the right to call me that." The words were slow and labored, and finished on a rasp as he ran out of air and strength.

Caitlin was suddenly so light-headed that she reached for the side rail of the bed for support and gripped it. Oblivious to her reaction, Jess fumbled with the oxygen tube.

The charged silence in the small space, punctuated by the blip and whir of machines, lent an eerie unreality to the scene. *He wanted a blood test.* Caitlin's mind was so stunned, so sluggish suddenly that the reason for her father's indifference—an indifference that so many times had flared out hatefully toward her—began to make sense only by slow degrees.

After a few reviving breaths, Jess's eyelids fluttered with relief, then fell shut. This time when he spoke, his words were slurred by weakness. "My blood inherits half the Broken B. Or Reno gets everything."

The effort made Jess struggle for air those next moments. His ongoing difficulty set off a small alarm that brought his nurse. Reno took her arm to pull her out of the way, but Caitlin resisted when he started to lead her from the room.

Somewhere beyond her shock it registered that Reno's touch was electrifying. When he tried a second time to lead her from the cubicle, she pulled away and retreated, her back to the glass wall as she watched the nurse examine her father.

The small crisis passed, and the monitors settled into an audible rhythm. The nurse turned toward them.

"He'll probably sleep now. It'd be better if you came back in a couple hours." She gave them both a faint smile, then waited for them to leave the cubicle ahead of her. Caitlin hesitated, then turned to make a swift exit. Reno followed at a more relaxed pace.

Once outside the ICU, she stalked to the elevators, escape the only clear thought in her mind. Her eyes were stinging with hurt, but the hot acid of old anger was boiling up like lava. Suddenly she was a child again, cast back into the abyss of her father's bewildering malevolence.

Her first stab at the elevator button missed. Frustrated, she jabbed at it again, then snatched her hand back when the button lit up.

"The lab's downstairs."

Reno's voice behind her made her jump.

Her low "Leave me alone," was instant. It was all she could do to contain her rising pain and fury.

The elevator bell sounded, but the door seemed to

take forever to open. When it did, she had to move aside and wait for the passengers to step off. She heard Reno enter the elevator after she did. They both turned to face the front of the car as the doors closed.

"The will says that your refusal to submit to a blood test to determine paternity will disqualify you from inheriting."

She heard Reno's grim tone and felt a fresh nick of pain. She covered her reaction with sarcasm.

"If the rightful heir loses out, Reno Duvall will be boss of the Broken B." She turned her head and glanced up at his unyielding profile. Her barb made no visible impression on him, and she was suddenly hot with resentment.

This was the man who—along with his spiteful brother and mother—had so easily won her father's love and regard. They'd been strangers when Jess had met them on a trip to San Antonio, strangers who'd meant more to Jess Bodine from day one than his own daughter had ever meant to him.

The Duvalls had gotten everything else that had rightfully belonged to her. She wouldn't let the last one get the Broken B, even if it was Reno. She'd have something of Jess's—and she'd glory in the fact that he'd go to his grave knowing he'd failed to deprive her of this last thing.

And yet, even when the blood test proved she was Jess's daughter, he'd fixed it so she'd receive only half the ranch. *Half!* He hadn't mentioned the oil holdings or the several businesses he'd acquired over the years.

Emotions that were suddenly as volatile to contain

as they were to identify, rose to an overwhelming pitch.

My blood inherits half the Broken B... Or Reno gets everything.

And what if the paternity test proved that Jess Bodine wasn't her biological father? Her furious vow to keep a Duvall from getting everything faltered.

Depression sent a chill over her. She looked away from Reno and stared at the closed doors in front of her.

Her memories of her mother were hazy. She remembered a beautiful, loving, dark-haired woman, but Elaina Chandler Bodine's face had blurred over the years. Caitlin recalled the funeral and how she'd later discovered that Jess had ordered all her mother's things taken away, and every picture of her in the house removed. Caitlin had been crushed when Jess had scolded her for her tears and her questions.

As an eight-year-old, she'd been grief-stricken and terrified by her mother's sudden death, but her father's refusal to comfort her or to allow his dead wife's name to be mentioned in his presence had deepened her trauma.

Though she could no longer clearly picture her mother's face, she remembered with aching clarity those days and weeks and months that had followed her death. She remembered the terror and monotony of stomachaches and nightmares, and her terrible loneliness when she'd wandered the house like a tiny ghost, searching for the love and comfort of her mother's presence.

That was when she'd become especially close to

her cousin, Madison. Madison had also lost her mother, though in a different way. Caitlin's mother had been taken from her by death; Maddie's mother had tired of her responsibilities and had dumped her on their grandmother, who'd lived nearby in town. Though Caitlin had always thought Maddie's loss was worse than her own because it was a personal rejection, at least Maddie's mother was alive somewhere, so she could have hope.

Their grandmother, Clara Chandler, had been almost as stern and unloving with Madison as Caitlin's father had been with her. The two young cousins had sought the solace and comfort of family from each other, and together they'd survived childhood. The same age, they'd formed a deep bond and, at times, they'd been as inseparable as twins.

Until Beau Duvall was killed, and Maddie—who'd been madly infatuated with him—believed as everyone else had, that Caitlin was responsible for his death.

"This is it."

Reno's gruff voice penetrated the fog of pain and memory. It took her a moment to realize that the elevator had stopped and the doors had slid open.

"To the right and down the hall." Reno's low murmur prodded her to move. She stepped forward and walked in the direction he'd indicated.

With every step she took, the dread she felt grew. She'd failed every other test her father's animosity and neglect had placed before her. Suddenly, she had no real confidence that she'd fare any better with this last one.

*   *   *

Caitlin walked into the heat of late afternoon. Her rental car was parked some distance from the hospital's main entrance, so she started toward it, reaching into her shoulder bag for the sunglasses she preferred to wear while driving.

She didn't know what had become of Reno. He'd vanished sometime after she'd filled out papers and was led to a room to have the blood sample drawn.

She rejected the idea of hanging around the hospital until her father was awake. After her first visit, she was certain there was no point in putting herself through a second one. If Jess Bodine had gone twenty-three years without softening toward his only child, she doubted that two hours would bring any significant change of heart.

The depression that had plagued her after her mother's death was suddenly as heavy and fresh as it had been back then, but Caitlin resisted it. That and the mercurial temper that seemed to go hand in hand with it. She'd matured in these last years, become solid emotionally. Life's little aggravations had no power over her. Her brief lapse after her father's bombshell was just that—a lapse, nothing more.

As she reached her car and got into its stifling interior, she thought again of Madison.

How close they'd been, sharing their angst and agonies, making their own good times, whether on Maddie's visits to the Broken B or during Caitlin's visits to their grandmother's mansion in Coulter City. No one cared when they wandered off, no one cared that they'd run wild, so long as they didn't annoy their guardians.

The worst thing about the aftermath of Beau's death was not that Caitlin had been banished from the Broken B. The worst thing had been how swiftly and completely Madison had turned against her. Maddie had known how much Caitlin had suffered, being supplanted by Beau. In the end, that knowledge had made it impossible for Caitlin to convince her lovesick cousin that she hadn't deliberately caused Beau's death. Madison had sided with everyone against her, and nothing Caitlin had been able to say convinced her otherwise.

The old gloom settled around her heart. Besides Jess and Maddie's absent mother, Rosalind, Maddie was her only living relative. The reminder deepened her sadness.

When Caitlin pulled her rental car out of the parking lot onto the street, she caught a glimpse of the interstate highway sign. She was tempted to pick up her things at the motel and drive back to San Antonio. She could catch a plane to Montana by tomorrow.

Her father would be dead soon, perhaps in a matter of hours. He was probably right about her not being his child. A man surely couldn't despise a child unless he was certain he had cause. She could drive away now and forget him and everything else, once and for all. She had nothing here, not even the Broken B. Now it would all go to Reno....

It was the thought of forever losing even a part of the ranch that finally made her go back to the motel with the intention of staying on in Coulter City.

The Broken B was home, such as it was. She'd missed the land, wild beautiful land that stretched for

forty thousand acres beneath the wide Texas sky.
Montana was beautiful, but Texas was home. The
ranch she'd worked on up north couldn't compare
with the deep attachment she still felt to the Broken
B.

The strong unbroken spirit she'd been blessed with
stirred forcefully. If she had any hope of getting even
a portion of what remained of her birthright, she had
to stay. The stubborn will that had helped her survive
the emotional devastation of her upbringing wouldn't
allow the thought of Jess Bodine denying her the
Broken B.

Even if the blood test went against her, surely the
fact that she'd been publicly claimed and raised as
Jess Bodine's legal child would give her some standing in the courts. She still had the large inheritance
from her grandmother at her disposal. If she had to,
she might be able to find the right lawyer and file suit
to contest the will. It might take years, but the thought
of thwarting Jess Bodine's last hateful deed was tan-
talizing.

Reno was the only member of his family worthy
of getting a piece of the Broken B, but if she had to,
she'd go to war with him to keep him from getting
it all.

CHAPTER TWO

RENO got out of his pickup and walked to the motel door. Number ten was Caitlin's room. There were out-of-state license plates on most of the nearby parked cars, but there were also two late-model rentals. One of those was probably hers.

Jess's condition had worsened, and the doctor told Reno it was time to notify his family. He'd called Madison St. John, Jess's niece, but she'd been vague about a last visit, particularly when he'd told her that Caitlin was back. He hadn't expected much from Madison. She wasn't the quiet, sweet kid she'd been before Beau's death. She was filthy rich now, spoiled by her money and her self-centered lifestyle, a social butterfly with iron wings and a razor tongue. It might be just as well if she stayed away from Jess.

Reno forgot about Madison St. John as he reached the door of number ten and knocked sharply. He'd tried to call Caitlin's room earlier, but there'd been no answer. It was past time for supper, so he assumed Caitlin had eaten. He damned sure hoped she had. He wasn't in the mood to take her anywhere but the hospital, and there wasn't much time.

He knocked again, louder this time, and was about to go back to the hospital without her when the door opened.

For a female who'd projected such poise and confidence earlier, Caitlin was surprisingly reluctant to open the door wider than a crack. He glimpsed the towel on her head and the skimpy robe she was wearing. He felt his lips move into an irritable line.

He wasted no time on preliminaries. "Get dressed." He stepped forward and pressed his hand on the door, but Caitlin pushed from her side to keep him from entering.

"Come back later." Her voice sounded breathless, as if she were a little afraid of him.

He pressed on the door hard enough to demonstrate that he meant business. "You don't have later. The doc says his time's close."

Reno watched the spasm of shock in her eyes. She immediately released the door and stepped back.

"I—I'd like to dry my hair," she said as she clutched the front of the short robe and took another step back. She was bare-legged from midthigh to her toes. Reno stepped inside and closed the door with a snap.

He could smell her shampoo and the clean scent of female skin. Without her usual jeans, work shirt and boots, Caitlin looked small and vulnerable. With her mane of hair hidden in the towel, nothing distracted his attention from her face.

And her eyes. Her lashes were black from the lingering dampness of her shower and her eyes were so blue they glowed like starlit sapphires. The natural beauty of her face took his breath away. The sight of her bare legs and his very male urge to see the rest of her bare made every nerve below his waist heat and tingle.

"Cover yourself."

His angry growl startled her into movement. She flitted away from him so suddenly that he was reminded of a fleeing doe. His gaze followed as she grabbed some clothes from an open suitcase. He didn't breathe normally until she shut herself in the bathroom.

Reno paced the room, furious with himself for his reaction, furious with her for affecting him so strongly.

He was fair-minded enough to acknowledge that she hadn't done anything improper, he had. He would never have forced his way into the bedroom of any scantily-clad female. He'd never had to. Why he'd pushed his way in on her when she wasn't decent defied reason.

Caitlin was dressed in a surprisingly short time. In moments she was out of the bathroom, tearing through one of her suitcases. Her hair was out of the towel and hung in wet disarray down her back. Reno gritted his teeth at the sight until her frantic movements made an impression on him. He could see her hands were shaking. She got a brush and a hair dryer, then dashed back to the bathroom. This time, she didn't bother to close the door.

Reno winced as she yanked the brush through her hair. That she was in an almighty hurry made him feel faint regret. He hated the turmoil she made him feel. Though he marshaled his anger by stoking his grudge against her, he could stand to let her punish her hair only a handful of strokes before he spoke up.

"No need to tear it out."

He'd barked the words and managed to startle her again. Her reaction reminded him of the past. Most of the time, Jess had only used one tone of voice with his daughter: harsh and loud. He'd never seemed to notice or care whether anyone else was around or not when he'd upbraided his only child. Reno ignored those times because Caitlin had sometimes deserved a scolding. He'd always assumed Jess spoke more kindly to her the rest of the time. But then, he'd lived on his own ranch near San Antonio before Beau's death, so he'd been around infrequently.

Why he suddenly questioned Jess's treatment of Caitlin irritated him. Jess hadn't been an especially affectionate man, but he'd doted on Beau and had been an attentive husband to their mother. Jess had been too good a man, too fair, to treat his daughter harshly without reason.

Caitlin continued to brush her hair, but she was only marginally less rushed about it. Moments later, she turned on the hair dryer.

Reno waited impatiently, although he was aware that no more than five minutes passed before she switched off the dryer and hastily brushed her hair again. When she finished, she hurried out of the bathroom and shoved the brush into her handbag. Neither of them spoke as they left the motel room.

You don't have later, Reno had said. The moment he'd spoken, Caitlin's refusal to allow her father another shot at her vanished. Jess might be moments from death. Now that the time had really come, and so suddenly, she was once again reduced to foolish hopes and impossible dreams.

Impending death had a profound effect on other people—she was certain it would on her—so perhaps it would have a positive effect on her father. The cynicism Jess Bodine had pounded into her warned that nothing had changed, but the hope she knew she'd have until her father took his last breath urged her to grab for this last chance.

She was shaking so hard when she tried to dig out the car key that she dropped it on the concrete and managed to kick it with her boot. She'd started to retrieve it when Reno stepped over and swung down to snatch it up.

"You're ridin' with me."

His gruff tone was harsh and sent her gaze streaking to his. The flat hard look he gave her hurt; the way his gaze shifted from hers communicated his reluctance to bother with her.

Too terrified to waste time arguing, she went with him to his truck. It surprised her when he opened the passenger door for her, then shut it once she was inside.

Her tension climbed higher as Reno drove swiftly through town to the hospital. He only paused for stop signs and red lights. Fortunately, at just after 9:00 p.m. Coulter City traffic was relatively light, so they pulled into the hospital parking lot in record time. It seemed to take forever to park and get into the hospital. By the time they reached the ICU floor, Caitlin's heart was pounding with anxiety.

They stepped off the elevator and were halfway down the hall when a doctor walked out of the ICU. Reno stopped and reached for her arm to halt her.

The doctor caught sight of them and approached. Caitlin read his somber expression and her heart fluttered sickeningly in her chest.

The doctor's quiet "I'm sorry," was directed to Reno before his kind dark eyes shifted to include Caitlin. "He passed away ten minutes ago."

The words caused a faint roaring in her ears. Her father was gone. The stifling numbness she felt helped her maintain her composure those next moments.

Reno was still gripping her arm when his fingers tightened. The hot current that radiated from his touch made a deep impression on her. The sudden human instinct to crowd close to that hot current, to somehow capture it and hold it close, made her reach for his hand.

The moment her fingers came in contact with his hard warm ones, she jerked her hand away. Confused by shock and appalled that the impulsive gesture had revealed her weakness, she tried to pull from his grip. His fingers flexed to hold her close while the doctor related an abridged version of her father's last moments.

The words "He went easy," stirred a restlessness that made it almost impossible for her to listen. When the doctor offered his condolences and quietly excused himself, she shuddered with relief.

Suddenly, Reno was leading her away. She walked along in a daze, dismayed by how unsteady she felt. They were alone in the elevator before she was fully aware of where he'd taken her. She pulled away to go back to the ICU, but he caught her as the doors slid shut.

Caitlin braced her hand against his chest. Her eyes were smarting and so blurred that his blue work shirt swam before her like a dark smear.

''I have to see him,'' she choked out, and somehow she lost her grip on the wild feeling she dimly recognized as hysteria. ''H-he can't be gone—not after he s-said those hateful things!''

She looked up through swimming eyes and tried to focus on Reno's harsh face. She clutched his shirt-front urgently. ''Those can't have been the only words—the only thing he had left to say—''

Reno's hands moved to her upper arms. The action registered, but she was losing control of herself too quickly. He gave her a small shake that jarred a sob out of her. The sound helped sober her and she bit her lip ruthlessly to stop the others.

She was coming apart in the presence of the man who hated her. God, what vicious pleasure he could take from her pain! Pride wouldn't allow this man—this man above all—to see her reduced to a pitiful heap of misery.

She tried to take a deep breath, but her throat was so swollen with pain that she could barely breathe. She tried to push away from him, but he held her too tightly.

They struggled briefly, and Caitlin realized his touch was burning her, sending sensual signals to every part of her body. But his refusal to release her so she could go to the ICU to see for herself that her father was really gone, tortured her.

It was irrational to fight him, but she did. He retaliated by backing her into the corner next to the elevator buttons. He released her arm only long enough to hit the stop button to bring the elevator to a bumping halt between floors.

Her gritted "Damn you—let me go!" only made him press harder. He wedged her lower body between his and the corner as his hands slid down her arms to her wrists. It was as if he'd read her mind and knew she was wild enough now to try to scratch him.

"It's over." Reno's voice was a rough murmur.

Caitlin shook her head emphatically. "He owed me something," she burst out. "Whether I'm his daughter or not, he was all I had."

She suddenly realized what she was saying and this time she bit her lip so hard she tasted blood. There was a rampage of fury and hurt inside. Repressing it was like trying to smother a forest fire with her bare skin. She shook uncontrollably, and the effort of holding back tears made her head pound.

"H-he was a cruel, unfeeling bastard." Hearing herself say the words aloud was shocking, and she took a series of deep breaths to calm herself before something worse came out of her mouth. She doubted Reno had ever glimpsed the man that she knew her father to be. She felt his surprise, sensed his strong disapproval.

Reno stared down into Caitlin's flushed, stricken face. She was shaking, but she held herself as stiffly as a fence post. Moments flew by in the silent elevator as he watched her struggle with her pain.

Though his heart was hard toward her and he believed she'd often deserved Jess's harsh treatment, it gave him no pleasure to witness her anguish. He hadn't approved of Jess's insistence on a blood test. On the other hand, Jess hadn't been completely rational the past couple of weeks. It was unfortunate that his last words to his daughter had been cruel.

The feel of her soft body trapped between his and the corner began to work on him. Their position— they were pressed together from waist to knee—was dangerously sexual.

Slowly he eased away from her until they were no longer touching. He still held her wrists, but the heat between them was scorching. He felt the stiffness seep from her body. She stared hard at his shirtfront, collecting herself. He sensed her strong will, her absolute determination to get control of herself. He couldn't help that he found a spark of admiration for that. The Caitlin Bodine of the past couldn't have summoned this control.

Satisfied with her progress, he released her wrists by slow degrees. The moment he was no longer touching her, she slipped from the corner. He pressed a button on the keypad and the elevator continued downward.

Caitlin didn't look directly at him again. She didn't speak to him either. The young woman who rode beside him in his truck to the motel was focused deeply inward, oblivious to everything outside her own wordless misery.

For the first time in five years, Caitlin awoke in her bedroom at the Broken B. Normally she was an early riser, but she glanced toward the alarm clock, surprised to see that it was almost 7:00 a.m.

Reno had brought her to the ranch. She'd been a zombie the night before. She dimly recalled watching him pack her things while she sat on the motel bed.

She hadn't protested when he'd taken over, she'd not had the will. As she lay in her bed and stared at the ceiling, she was amazed that he'd taken care of her. It was absolutely stunning that he'd brought her to the Broken B when he hated her so.

Perhaps it proved that Reno wasn't as heartless as her father after all. Perhaps he didn't hate her as intensely as she'd thought.

The moment the notion entered her mind, she shoved it away. Reno blamed her for his brother's death. How could he not hate her? In light of how he felt, the mystery of why he'd taken such good care of her and brought her home was baffling.

It was too much to sort out. She got up and dressed, then went downstairs. The realization that she was finally home put tremendous pressure on her battered emotions. She almost retreated to her room before she reminded herself that she had to face everything eventually.

Quietly, she wandered through the massive ranch house. She knew every inch of it, and it was a comfort to see that nothing much had changed. Her father had spent most of his waking hours out-of-doors, so she associated the house more with her memories of her mother than with him. Reno's mother had changed almost nothing.

Now that Jess was dead, she thought about her mother's pictures. Had Jess destroyed them, or merely packed them away someplace? She didn't think he'd given them to her grandmother, since she'd never mentioned them. The idea that they might still be in the house somewhere, hidden, made her determined to find them.

She walked into the back hall on her way to the kitchen for breakfast when Reno came down the hall from the other end and met her there.

His eyes were intent on her face, searching, assessing. "You look better this morning."

She stiffened as his blue gaze ran down her slender body. She saw the male interest in the look and felt faintly threatened. Once, she'd have given anything to attract Reno's interest. Now it made her uneasy. Anger gleamed in his gaze. Clearly, his attraction to her infuriated him. She didn't speak.

"Mary's waitin' breakfast."

The news surprised her. "Mary? Isn't Corrie around anymore?"

"Corrie retired last year. Hannah, too, the year before that," he told her.

Corrie and Hannah had been the cook and housekeeper since just after her mother's death. A part of her was relieved. Hannah had never seemed to approve of her. Both women had been charmed by Beau, though they hadn't cared much for his mother. In the two weeks after Beau's death before Caitlin had been banished, they'd been distant with her. She'd always believed they'd blamed her for Beau's death. Like everyone else.

Reno waited for her to step forward and precede him to the kitchen.

Mary was a warm, friendly woman, who seemed

pleased to be introduced to Caitlin. She offered her condolences to them both. Caitlin was less tense then, but she was surprised when Reno joined her at the kitchen table for breakfast.

When Mary set two heaped plates of food before them, the appetite Caitlin was certain she couldn't muster began to stir.

She picked up her fork and had a bite of the fluffy scrambled eggs. When Mary left the kitchen, she glanced Reno's way and caught him staring at her. She read the traces of hostility in his gaze. He probably hated sitting across the table from her. She was suddenly so self-conscious that the bite of food stuck in her throat. His blue gaze dropped to watch her swallow, then went dark.

Caitlin rested her fork on her plate, her meager appetite fleeing beneath his scrutiny.

"When's the funeral?" Her soft question distracted him and he focused on his own meal.

"Day after tomorrow."

Neither of them spoke again while they ate. Caitlin eventually relaxed enough to force down a few more bites of food. Reno finished and leaned back with what was left of his coffee.

"I'd like to see the ranch." Her statement brought his gaze back to hers. She endured a long burning look. She could tell the instant her request reminded him of Beau's death. His eyes darkened again and went hard.

"You've got funeral arrangements to make."

The blunt reminder made her uncomfortable. "You've been closer to him than anyone," she said quietly. "I'm sure he'd prefer that you handled things."

"You're his daughter."

Caitlin gripped her coffee cup. She dared to meet his gaze squarely. "You and Beau were the sons he always wanted, but was cheated of. Until he married your mother."

The blue fire in his eyes was pure hatred.

"Don't speak Beau's name to me."

The low rumble of his voice hit her chest like a sledgehammer. The pain was so intense that she had to focus on breathing slowly in, then out, to relieve it.

"Why did you bring me home?" The words came out in a whisper.

He stared over at her, his enmity shining out like a laser. "Maybe to prove that you and I can't live here, even if you can inherit."

"So you're after your pound of flesh," she stated dully.

"It'll take more than a pound to even the score."

He didn't bother now to conceal his hatred for her. She was shaking all over and held herself stiffly to hide it. The impulse to defend herself made her incautious.

"You never wanted to hear what happened."

"I'm not much for lies."

The accusation was so insulting—Caitlin *never* lied—that her temper shot skyward. Her low "Go to hell, Reno," was heartfelt.

His quiet "Been there," pinned the blame squarely on her. She rallied to deflect it.

"So have I."

The air thundered with hate. The injustice of it left her raw inside. The wall of rage between them was miles high and so wide that nothing would ever overcome it. The thought was overwhelming. The knowledge that there was nothing she could do to change things sent her spirits into a downward slide.

She tossed her napkin to the table and rose. "Make the funeral arrangements. I'm going for a ride."

She didn't look directly at Reno, but she felt his gaze cut at her. Hating her.

She went to her room briefly for her hat, then escaped the house through the front door to avoid coming face-to-face with Reno.

As she walked through the yard toward the corrals and barns, she noticed that most things looked just the same. She entered the stable and immediately recognized a couple of the horses. She didn't relish meeting any of the men. The three cowboys who had testified on her behalf at the inquest were nowhere to be seen.

On the other hand, all three were older men. The oldest, Lucky Reed, the cowboy who'd been her champion, had probably retired by now. She finished her brief inspection of the horses still at the stable, then selected one.

Her father's saddle was still in the tack room. She got it and a bridle, then carried them to the horse she'd chosen.

The black gelding had been her father's favorite. He'd been a lively four-year-old five years ago. Now he seemed calmer, more like the competent working horse her father would have expected.

Caitlin led him out of the stall, gave him a quick grooming, then saddled him. Excitement made her hurry. Memories of the land she'd missed so much—and her private place—pulled at her. The only real peace she'd known growing up had been on the land. The only true comfort she'd had was the comfort of her private place.

She belonged to the land. She'd not had a secure place in her family, but she'd had a place on the land. The wildness of it connected with something wild in her. She relished the seasons, was sensitive to their cycles. She knew her place out there, felt herself fit into the universe somehow. Though she was a mere speck on the landscape, she was part of it.

As she rode out of the stable and past the outbuildings and corrals, something shifted inside her, and she felt herself slip naturally into the panorama of range land before her.

The black felt solid beneath her and he obeyed her slightest signal. His well-trained response heightened her sense of control, of dominance. She might never handle her personal life or the tricky relationships she was bound to with any real skill or success, but she had an affinity for animals, and a natural competence with them that made her feel settled and sure of herself.

She rode on for nearly an hour before she angled in a new direction. She couldn't bear to go near the canyon where Beau had died, so she'd altered her path to avoid it. She ended up north of the old cabin and changed direction again to ride to it.

Caitlin thought of it as a cabin, but it was the adobe ruin of a turn-of-the-century homestead. Most of the old roof had rotted and fallen in, or had been blown away. Years ago, she'd hauled in enough lumber to construct a crude roof near the chimney. The two layers of wood with a layer of tarp in between had provided shade from the sun and protection enough from the rain. The adobe was crumbled and weathered down, but the irregular walls were still high enough to count as shelter from the wind.

The moment she saw it, she felt relief. It still looked the same as she remembered. When she reached the old structure, she dismounted, loosening the saddle cinch before she led the black to the east side of the ruin.

She inspected the small lean-to, then led the horse in out of the hot sun and removed his saddle. When she came out, she walked to the front of the cabin to the wide space where the door had once been and stepped inside.

The sparrows that had built a nest under the crude roof burst out and shot through the open space overhead into the sky. If any other animals had moved in, they'd already fled. Caitlin made a cursory check for snakes, then carefully checked the old fireplace chimney.

Because she hadn't been there to light a fire in the past five years, at least one family of birds was nesting in the old adobe. She heard their flutters and chirps, but didn't disturb them. She walked around the limited confines, then took up a place at the deep dip in the wall where a window had once been.

The magic of the place began to ease over her. Thoughts about her father, Reno and Beau began to crowd in, but they seemed manageable here.

Her father's demand for a blood test explained his treatment of her over the years. Jess Bodine had been uncompromising on the subject of loyalty and fidelity—to *him*. He'd proved at the inquest how little loyalty he'd felt toward his daughter. Though Caitlin had been too young to know about such things when her mother was alive, it wouldn't surprise her to discover that her father was the one who'd been unfaithful.

Had her mother been unfaithful? A man as proud as her father couldn't have tolerated even the hint that his wife had cheated on him. Clearly, he'd never been able to separate his feelings for his daughter from his suspicion that she might not be his.

The fact that he'd treated her so poorly was inexcusable. A child—even if it had been her—shouldn't have to bear the brunt of a man's anger toward his wife.

Eventually, her thoughts turned to Beau. Beau had been a charmer and a daredevil. He'd also possessed a wide streak of cruelty that he'd often displayed with animals and with her. But he'd also been clever enough to conceal the cruel things he'd done from Jess and from Reno.

She doubted Reno had ever known about his brother's dark side. Beau had idolized his older brother and had behaved well around Reno to impress him. Privately, Beau had reveled in the fact that his mother favored him over her older son. Sheila Duvall Bodine had a penchant for spoiling her youngest, giving him anything he wanted, laughing over his pranks and laying into anyone who might take exception to anything her favorite said or did.

Caitlin had never been impressed by Beau's charm or his handsome looks. When he managed to skillfully play to her father's desire for a son and completely dominated Jess's time and attention, she'd hated Beau for upstaging her. Her father finally had the male child he'd resented not having, and he'd completely lost interest in his daughter.

It had been terrible to see her father bond so instantly and completely to his new wife and her ten-year-old son. The three of them became the close, devoted family Caitlin had hungered all her life to be a part of. It'd been agony to be excluded from that.

Reno was ten years older than Beau and he'd run his family's ranch for years. Caitlin noticed right away that he'd also been excluded from the tight unit his mother and brother had formed with Jess. Nevertheless, Jess had treated Reno as an equal, and their relationship had been a good, solid one.

It had never seemed to trouble Reno that his mother and brother's lives were bound so obsessively close to Jess's. He'd had his own life and a strong self-image that seemed to make him impervious to the trials and heartaches of lesser mortals.

Caitlin had been instantly attracted to that. Reno seemed strong and tough and very nearly indestructible. He'd also paid attention to her.

Not a lot—he made sure he kept her at arm's

length. But when he was around he saw to it that she was included. He made it a point to draw her out in conversation or to make some kind remark to her or on her behalf. She'd noticed immediately how much better her father treated her when Reno was around, and she'd always looked forward to Reno's visits.

By the time she'd turned seventeen, she'd had a crush on him. She must have been too obvious about it, because it was about that time that Reno's attitude toward her began to cool. She'd suffered the loss of his attention, suffered the misery of knowing that the desperate flaw inside her had driven away another person who'd been important in her life. Reno's heart had closed to her almost as completely as her father's had, and it had devastated her to realize how alike he and her father were.

A year later when Beau was killed, Reno had stood solidly against her. He'd taken the lead in ostracizing her, refusing to let her speak to him, then having her barred from Beau's funeral. She was certain he'd played a major part in her exile, though it had been his mother who'd demanded that.

If Sheriff Juno hadn't stepped in on her behalf, she was certain she would have been arrested and jailed. The inquest had been traumatic enough to go through. The fact that the testimony of witnesses had absolved her of wrongdoing made no impression on Jess or his wife, and certainly hadn't on Reno, who'd not been present for some of the most critical testimony. All of them, along with Maddie, had turned their backs on her. In the face of such blame, Caitlin couldn't have stayed on in Coulter City.

She'd taken her inheritance from her grandmother, who'd died several weeks before Beau, and wandered for months like a lost soul. She'd ended up in Montana, working on a dude ranch that had recently been converted into a summer camp for troubled teens. Though she'd signed on as a horse wrangler and taught several of the kids to ride, emotionally she'd fit right in with the ones who'd been sent there by social workers or the courts.

Being around the kids who'd come through the SC Ranch helped her to come to terms with the emotional deprivation she'd grown up with. As painful and lonely as her childhood had been, the kids who came to the SC had lived through even tougher times. Her own emotional abuse and neglect seemed mild compared to the abuse several of the ranch kids had suffered. She understood their anger and she'd learned how to manage her own by watching many of them struggle to master theirs. The ones who'd failed left the ranch with only a remote chance of ever making a decent life for themselves. Those were the kids— the failures—who'd terrified her into getting a grip on herself.

Coming back to Coulter City and the Broken B had been the severe test that had jarred her into realizing how far she still had to go.

The peace of the old homestead eventually stilled her troubled thoughts. It was late afternoon before she saddled the gelding and led him out of the lean-to. She mounted and started back to the ranch headquarters at a sedate walk.

CHAPTER THREE

RENO watched Caitlin ride to the stable. She held herself erect, her eyes on the barn as if she didn't notice the few ranch hands at work in the corrals.

Now he noted the horse she rode—Jess's favorite—and that she'd used Jess's saddle. He bit back his irritation. There hadn't been many horses at the stable that day. Not many extra saddles in the tack room either. Caitlin was an excellent horsewoman and a good judge of horseflesh. The black gelding was one of the best horses still at the stable, so her choice might have been more a natural one than a symbolic one.

Why he suddenly wanted to give her the benefit of the doubt aggravated him.

But then, he also had mixed feelings about the outcome of the blood test. Now that he knew Jess had doubted his daughter's paternity, he had to admit that Caitlin didn't favor Jess much at all. He'd heard she was the image of her mother, and she must be because she resembled Jess so little.

It was a fresh surprise for him to realize that he didn't want her to lose every claim to Jess's estate. She'd been raised as Jess's daughter, whatever the circumstances of her birth. Jess should never have made her inheritance conditional on something she'd been innocent of.

Even he had to admit that Jess had been brutally unfair. It would have been more honest, more merciful for Jess to have disowned her long ago and left her out of the will completely.

When Reno realized the track his thoughts were on, and how far they'd gone, he felt a rush of anger. He watched her reach the stable and dismount. The painful turbulence she made him feel clouded his mind with dark thoughts.

She moved with a regal grace that drew the eye and stirred the imagination. The memory of what she'd looked like in that skimpy robe the night before sent a gust of heat through him. No woman in his life had affected him this strongly and he'd had enough of them to know the difference.

Once Caitlin led the gelding into the stable, he found himself stalking toward it. He caught up with her just as she pulled the saddle and turned to carry it to the tack room.

"Where were you?"

Caitlin hesitated at Reno's gruff demand. She'd known he'd show up the moment she got in. She'd prepared herself, but the accusation in his tone sent a quiver of hurt and wariness through her. She didn't glance up at his face, but stepped around him to continue to the tack room.

Her soft "Staying out of your way," was as much of a nonanswer as she dared. She felt his anger spike high as she stepped into the tack room and stored the saddle. She walked out—still not looking at Reno— and began to give the gelding a quick brushing.

Silence crackled between them while she finished

with the horse and led him into his stall. Her unease multiplied as she got the horse a measure of grain, checked his water, then stepped out of the stall and closed the gate.

As if he meant to keep a close watch on her, Reno tolerated the wait. Caitlin wasn't certain what to do next. His silent anger intimidated her, but she struggled not to show it and started up the stable aisle for the house.

Reno fell into step beside her. Though neither of them spoke, the tension between them was taut. By the time they walked into the kitchen, Caitlin's stomach was in knots.

How could she live on the Broken B with Reno? She knew right away that she'd hate living day in and day out with his enmity. And yet, until she found out for certain if she qualified to inherit half the ranch, she had no choice but to put up with it.

She didn't relish getting into a battle of wills with him on a permanent basis, but if she had to, she would. There was always the chance he'd allow her to talk about Beau's death. It might make some small difference, though what she could tell him had just as much potential to make him hate her more as it did to neutralize his hostility.

Still, depending on the outcome of the blood test, she wouldn't walk on eggshells around Reno. She'd had enough of that with her father.

They left their hats on wall pegs and washed up. Caitlin used the sink in the kitchen while Reno used the one in the bathroom off the back hall. They both arrived in the dining room just as Mary finished setting the food on the table. As if the pleasant-natured cook sensed the hostility in the silence between them, she ducked back into the kitchen.

Caitlin took her place across the long, polished table from Reno. Neither of them sat in the ornate chair at the head. Mary had set their places to the left and right of the big chair. The fact that they'd have to eat facing each other didn't do wonders for her appetite, but Caitlin sat down and reached for her napkin.

Reno's low voice split the silence. "Visitation is tomorrow night at seven. Funeral's at 10:00 a.m. the day after."

Caitlin couldn't help that her gaze shifted up to meet his. Reno was watching her so closely that she felt like a moth on a pin. His dark brows were slanted at a disapproving angle.

"Would you prefer that I skip the visitation…and the funeral?" Her soft question made his expression go black.

"You'll go to both. And you'll play the part of the bereaved daughter."

The low words cut at her. She dropped her gaze to her plate. "My acting abilities are limited."

"Just show up, keep to yourself, and keep your mouth shut."

Stung by his edict, she toyed with her fork for a moment, but didn't pick it up. "I'll attend the funeral and the graveside service, but not the visitation."

At the funeral and graveside service, she would be spared having to make small talk with community members who, no doubt, thought of her as a murderess. The visitation was a much more social occasion, and it was easy to picture herself being snubbed and treated like an outcast. Not to mention having to come face-to-face with others like Reno, who simply couldn't conceal their hatred. Beau had charmed and won over a lot of people in the eight years he'd lived on the Broken B.

"You'll go to the visitation." The low rumble of Reno's voice was final.

Caitlin lifted her gaze to his furious one. "You know what everyone thinks of me."

"You were raised as Jess's daughter. You won't dishonor his memory by staying away." He paused. "Whatever else they think, you earned."

She couldn't look away from his harsh expression.

"How many people know about the paternity test?" She watched his gaze flicker slightly.

"Jess didn't make a public announcement."

Caitlin heard instantly what Reno didn't say. Jess might not have made it public, but everyone knew about it anyway.

Her gaze fell, and the sickness that stole over her made her weak. Moments slid by as she tried to push back the melancholy she felt. Finally, her fingers numb, she pulled her napkin off her lap and lifted it to the table. She got up without a word and walked from the room.

The moment Caitlin placed her napkin beside her plate and rose, Reno felt a powerful stroke of guilt. The low swearword that burst from his lips was quiet, but heartfelt.

Caitlin walked to her room in a haze of fresh pain. Jess's cruelty—even though he was dead—had just as much potential to destroy her as it always had. She'd been back in Coulter City little more than twenty-four hours and Jess had already spoiled her hope of being able to stay on peacefully.

And now everyone knew he believed she was a bastard.

Caitlin walked into her bathroom and removed her clothes, hoping a hot shower would lift her spirits. She stayed under the needle-sharp spray so long that the water eventually began to cool.

Finally she turned off the taps and stepped out. The huge towel she used pleasantly abraded her skin. When she finished drying off, she wrapped the towel around herself from shoulder to thigh and pulled it tight.

She craved the comfort of being wrapped so securely. The hunger to be close to another human being warred with her secret terror of allowing anyone to get close.

The paradox was the torment of her life. There'd been a few times when she'd given in to the craving and dated in hopes of finding someone to love. But the moment a kiss or embrace began to progress to something more, she'd backed away.

She'd never been touched by real passion. She'd never understood why feverish kisses and groping embraces left her unmoved. Eventually, she'd come to the conclusion that she was frigid. The reminder made her pull the towel tighter for a few moments more before she unwrapped it and reached for her robe.

The stress of the past twenty-four hours had exhausted her. She brushed her teeth, worked the tangles from her hair, and methodically dried it. By the time she finished, it was just past 7:00 p.m. It didn't matter that the sun hadn't gone down yet. Sleep was too compelling a notion to resist.

Caitlin reached the side of her bed and pulled back the comforter and top sheet when a sharp knock sounded on the door. She could tell right away who it was. Only Reno's knock could sound that demanding.

She made certain her robe was belted securely, then turned toward the door. "What do you want?"

"Mary kept your supper warm."

Caitlin's lips parted in surprise. The low words were gruff, but she knew Reno well enough to detect the hint of softness behind them.

Memories of his visits to the Broken B when she was a child slipped past her fatigue. Those few golden recollections of the times Reno had been kind to her stung her eyes and swamped her with nostalgia.

She stepped silently to the door and placed a shaking hand on the smooth wood. She rested her forehead against the wall next to it and tried to sound unaffected.

"I was on my way to bed. I'll thank her in the morning."

Silence.

Then, "Open the door."

The low order made her lift her head and reach for the doorknob. Hurt and sudden anger made her yank the door open

"What's wrong? Didn't you get in your quota of hateful remarks today?"

Because she'd been unable to meet his eyes those first seconds, she'd looked past him. A heartbeat later, it registered that he was holding a tray. The sight of her untouched food shocked her. Her gaze sped up to his solemn expression.

Reno silently cursed the guilt that had prompted him to take her supper to her. If he'd thought he'd catch her in that skimpy little robe, he would have lived with the guilt or bothered Mary to bring her the tray.

And if he'd thought he'd see the shock on Caitlin's face when she'd noticed the tray, or that he'd witness the faint trace of hope that brightened the dull sheen of her eyes, he would have ignored the impulse completely.

He stalked past her with the tray and carried it straight to the low chest at the foot of her bed. He set it down and turned.

Caitlin had barely moved. Her eyes searched his with an intensity that signaled her confusion.

Compelled to discourage her from reading anything hopeful into his action, he murmured a low "Mary's feelings might be hurt."

Caitlin's gaze fell to the food tray. He sensed that her fragile hope fell just as far. While her attention was on the tray, his attention was drawn to her glossy mantle of dark hair. It streamed around her shoulders and arms, and hung past her softly rounded hips, creating a beautiful frame for her perfect body.

Reno's gaze followed downward, and he felt himself respond. Hatred had no power over his libido. Lust made him realize he was weakening toward her. And because disloyalty was anathema to him, his gut churned with self-disgust.

Caitlin looked up from the tray to Reno's face. His expression was as hard as she'd ever seen it. Already he regretted this minor kindness. She tensed in self-protection. Normal courtesy made her offer a quiet "Thank you."

Time seemed to stop as they stared at each other. Neither of them moved. When Reno's blue gaze made a slow, lingering journey from her face to her toes, she felt a peculiar heat follow all the way down. The room was suddenly stifling, and her heart pumped wildly. When his gaze returned to hers, her breath caught in her throat.

Reno started toward her and she immediately shied from the door. His gaze shifted away from her as he walked past.

The moment he was gone, she quickly closed the door. The restless ache she felt left her trembling in the silent room as she listened to his boot steps recede.

At first, the visitation was a small nightmare. It seemed nearly everyone in their part of Texas had turned out for it. Caitlin stood woodenly and endured the brief hellos and stiff nods. None of the few who actually approached her to express condolences lingered to speak with her.

Most of the Broken B ranch hands filed through the throng of townspeople, oilmen and cattlemen who filled the large parlor of the funeral home. Caitlin recognized many of them. Each ranch hand acknowledged her presence with a polite nod as they passed. Several feet down the line, she saw the three older cowboys who'd testified on her behalf at the inquest.

A wave of emotion and relief made her eyes fill and she blinked determinedly. She endured an agony of suspense as she waited for the three to reach her.

Would they acknowledge her in any more than the most minimal way? Had time and community disapproval changed their attitudes toward her?

Their testimony had legally absolved her of guilt in Beau's death, but she'd never been certain how much they'd seen. Her father had isolated her from everyone after that day, so she'd never been able to learn whether they'd also witnessed the foolish act that had precipitated Beau's death.

Lucky Reed was the first of the three to reach her. Bob Wilson and Tar Bailey followed. Their weathered faces were solemn, befitting the occasion.

Lucky offered a callused hand—he was the first person all evening to actually extend his hand to her—and Caitlin reached gratefully to clasp it.

"Hope yer meanin' to stay on, Miz Caitlin. The Broken B's yer birthright."

It didn't escape her notice that Lucky didn't remark on her father's death or offer condolences. And as she looked into his kind, brown eyes, she saw the loyalty and sympathy he'd always conferred on her. Lucky, more than anyone, had witnessed her father's harshness toward her, and Beau's cruelty. And because he'd been a man her father had respected, his frequent defense of her had gotten him nothing more punitive than a cussing or cow camp duty on another part of the ranch.

Privately, Caitlin had always believed that many of the Broken B's ranch hands might have quit if Lucky had been fired. Her father had been savvy enough to know that his harshness with his employees had caused most of them to feel more loyal to his top hand than they did to him. She'd never been close enough to Jess to know how deeply he might have resented that fact.

She gave the old ranch hand a smile that trembled slightly. Her soft "Thank you, Lucky," was choked.

The old man placed his free hand over the back of hers in a rare show of affection. His voice went lower. "Duvall's a fair man. He'll come around in time."

Now her eyes did sting. Emotions that were so powerful she could barely contain them made her clasp Lucky's hands with both of hers.

"Yes, about the time Broken B cows give birth to purple Holsteins." The wild exaggeration made the old cowhand give her a sad smile.

"If that's true, you'll be around long enough to see the Broken B switch over to a dairy operation." His face went solemn again. "Yer mama was a fine, churchgoin' lady. Jess had no cause to doubt her."

A single tear hovered on her lash and she jerked up a hand to dash it away. She could only mouth the words, "Thank you."

"Anything you need, anyone troubles you, you let me or Bob or Tar know."

Lucky's gruff pledge was echoed by the other two

men who filed up to shake her hand and show their respect. The three men lingered with her the rest of the evening in a silent demonstration of loyalty.

Eventually, Caitlin's emotions settled. She'd made it a point all evening to make certain she never looked Reno's way, so she had no idea how he was taking things with Lucky and the others. Her cousin, Madison, never put in an appearance.

It was a profound relief when the visitation ended and the crowd melted away. Reno must have gone out with everyone else, because Lucky and the others were the last to leave.

Caitlin lingered alone in the flower-decked room. She glanced toward the casket and didn't realize until she stopped beside it that she'd crossed to it.

In death, her father's features were less harsh. Though his long illness had dramatically changed his appearance, there were strong traces of the man he'd once been.

The grief she hadn't allowed herself since the night he'd died settled heavily on her heart. Though the mystery of her father's rejection now had an explanation, she was still tormented by it. The knowledge that Jess had never felt remorse for his treatment of her, had never been interested enough in her welfare to consider her feelings or care about the impact of his actions on her life, had left a gaping hole in her heart and psyche. He hadn't valued anything about her, and had gone out of his way to punish her for the sin he believed her mother had committed against him. Lucky believed her mother was innocent. If she had been, it compounded the tragedy of her upbringing.

A large part of her suddenly hoped she wasn't Jess's biological daughter. Because it was less painful to think she'd been rejected by a man who wasn't her real father than by the one who was, she found herself clinging to the irrational hope that the blood test would be negative.

In those moments beside the casket, she acknowledged to herself that it might be more important to the child she had been to fail the blood test than it was to inherit the Broken B.

Finally, she made herself leave the silent room. She walked out of the funeral parlor to her rental car and got in for the long lonely ride to the ranch.

Reno stood next to the liquor cabinet in the den of the ranch house and poured himself a whiskey.

He didn't disapprove of the old ranch hands' demonstration of loyalty and support for Caitlin. He knew that Lucky had always come to Caitlin's defense. Over the years, he'd heard Jess disparage Lucky's interference, but he'd tolerated it.

Lucky, Bob, and Tar were scrupulously honest men, so Reno completely believed what he'd heard about their testimony concerning Caitlin's failed efforts to save Beau—though he firmly believed she was responsible for Beau's death.

The judge hadn't given strong consideration to testimony about the history of the conflict between Caitlin and Beau. Instead, he'd focused on testimony about what the three men had seen from a distance as they'd ridden toward the flood-swollen canyon.

According to what he'd heard of Lucky's account, Caitlin had been lying a few feet from the lip of the canyon, with Beau standing between her and the water's edge. In their mad ride to reach the two, the riders galloped their horses into a ripple of land, so their view had been obscured for a few precious seconds.

By the time they charged over the hill, a six-by-ten-foot chunk of earth was dropping into the current. Beau had flung himself toward Caitlin to keep from falling in, but she was scrambling backward as the sod beneath her legs slid away.

Beau had caught her ankle as she scrambled backward but, according to the three cowboys, the water had surged up and Beau's grip had either slipped off her boot or the force of the water had torn him away.

Though Lucky had testified that Caitlin had barely escaped being dragged in with Beau, Reno's mother believed that Caitlin had deliberately kicked off Beau's grip on her ankle. Sheila Bodine had stood up and declared that at the inquest before the judge had rapped his gavel and called for order. His mother had become hysterical then, screaming that Lucky was lying to protect Caitlin. The judge had ordered Sheila removed from the courtroom. Reno had escorted her out and the inquest had proceeded.

Though Reno believed Lucky and the others had given truthful testimony, he thought their loyalty to Caitlin might have colored their interpretation of what they'd seen. Because they were still a distance away when the bank crumbled and Beau caught her ankle, Caitlin hadn't been aware of their approach. It was logical for her to believe she could get away with kicking Beau's hand off her ankle.

Because word of Sheila's outburst had gotten around, her interpretation of what Caitlin had done—deliberately kicking to break her rival's hold on her—ended up being the version most people believed. Everyone knew about the bitter feud between Caitlin and Beau. Most people had sympathized with Caitlin, but when Beau was killed and Sheila demanded an arrest, people began to believe Caitlin might be guilty. After the inquest, when Jess threw Caitlin off the Broken B, everyone took it as a sign that even Jess Bodine himself believed his daughter had escaped the punishment of the law.

But he'd heard that testimony had also revealed her wild race to her horse, then her dogged chase along the edge of the swift-running flood waters to throw Beau a rope. The riders had been too far away for her to hear their shouts or the hoofbeats of their horses over the roar of the water, so her efforts then must have been genuine.

Unless she'd suddenly realized what she'd done by kicking Beau away and was frantic to rectify her rash act.

When Beau had been struck by a flood-driven tree branch and disappeared beneath the surface of the dark water, Caitlin had given up trying to drag back the rope for another try. She'd vaulted off her horse and had been about to plunge into the flood water after Beau, when Lucky reached her and all but tackled her to keep her from jumping in. It had taken all three men to restrain her.

Later, they'd found Beau's body miles down the river. The power of the water had torn most of his clothes off. The flood-driven debris had so battered him that he'd been almost unrecognizable. Reno was the one who'd identified his body.

The stark horror of it still haunted him and he tossed back the whiskey, hoping for the fiery burn to distract him from the memory.

Grief had taken a toll on them all, but his mother had suffered it the strongest. Unable to bear the death of her youngest son, she'd lost her mind soon afterward. Her days settled into a pattern of listlessness, punctuated by exhausting hours of rage. She rarely ate and rarely slept. She either wandered the house at all hours in a daze, or she locked herself in her room and screamed. Most of her rage had been directed toward Caitlin. But sometimes, when she was at her worst, she'd blamed Reno.

Reno had accepted long ago that Beau was his mother's favorite son. Mother and son had been unusually close. Because he'd had to bear the responsibility of the family ranch after his father's death when he was seventeen, Reno hadn't been able to be a close part of the relationship between his mother and brother.

He hadn't approved of the fact that his mother spoiled his kid brother with attention and affection, but he'd kept silent. Sheila had had a difficult time with his father's death, and he'd figured her focus on Beau was her way of coping.

He'd overlooked his own hurt. At seventeen, he'd considered himself too much a man to be petted and spoiled like his seven-year-old brother.

Over the years, his mother had come to see him as an authority figure and provider rather than a true son. After Beau's death, he became aware of how vast the distance between him and his mother had grown when she began to blame him for being the son who was still alive.

He'd never forget her first screaming fury when she'd turned on him, slapped his face, and cursed him for being alive while Beau laid cold in his grave.

After that, Jess had gotten her professional help. In the months that followed, she'd been in and out of the Coulter City hospital psychiatric ward. And though she began to have times when she seemed lucid, she'd never truly recovered.

On the last day of her life, she'd flown into another wild rage. The heart problems that had recently developed made her susceptible to the sudden heart attack that killed her. But not before she'd cursed him one last time for not being the son she'd had to bury.

They found out later that she'd been hiding her medication instead of taking it, which explained the intensity of her last outburst. But nothing, not even the abnormal extent of her grief, excused her blaming him for being alive.

Reno reached for the whiskey decanter and poured himself another drink.

Surely it was the injustice of what his mother had done to him that made him feel this odd sympathy for Caitlin. The more he remembered about his visits to the Broken B years ago, the more he began to wonder just how harshly Jess had treated her when he wasn't around. Jess's demand for proof of paternity was as cruel as Reno's mother's wish that he had died instead of Beau. Perhaps that accounted for this slow softening toward Caitlin.

What had Lucky and the others seen that day? Had Caitlin kicked Beau away on purpose, or had his hand slipped off her wet boot? Could the instinct to save herself have been so strong that she'd kicked off Beau's grip to keep from being dragged into the raging current?

Whatever had happened, it was a fact that Caitlin was the reason Beau had been at the canyon. If everyone hadn't worried about her going out alone at a dangerous time, Beau wouldn't have been out trying to find her. If she'd been at the house where she belonged, instead of pouting, Beau would still be alive.

This time, the whiskey went down hot, but without the fire. It did nothing to blunt the turmoil inside him.

CHAPTER FOUR

AT THE funeral, Reno, Caitlin, and her cousin, Madison, sat in the secluded alcove reserved for family. Reno sat between the two cousins. That Reno sat anywhere near Caitlin surprised her.

Unless it was to prevent gossip. On the other hand, it seemed to Caitlin that Reno's sitting next to her would cause more gossip than if he'd maintained a physical distance.

She struggled not to read anything hopeful into his actions. He'd been remote with her that day, though his hostility seemed to have eased. It might simply be that all his attention was on the funeral. It made sense that he was the only true mourner in the family alcove, since his relationship with Jess had been a good one.

Madison didn't speak to Caitlin. Instead, she maintained a frosty silence that warned Caitlin not to address her directly. Her cousin's ability to treat her as a nonentity compounded the melancholy she felt.

Madison had grown into a very beautiful woman. She'd lightened her blond hair and now dressed chicly. Her expertly made-up face and perfectly manicured nails hinted at an obsession with her looks. There was no sign of the shy tomboy she'd once been.

Her frigid blond beauty contrasted with Caitlin's dark coloring, but their eyes were the same jewel

blue, and they shared the same patrician features that
marked them as family.

Caitlin thought about her mother's pictures, which
she'd been unable to find at the ranch. Did she dare
ask Madison if they'd been among their grandmother's things? Would Madison even acknowledge
the question?

The service seemed to take forever. Caitlin sat dry-
eyed throughout, though she felt the heavy pressure
of grief. When the service was over, Reno directed
them to the funeral car for family that would follow
the hearse.

Madison declined the ride in the family car, and
slid into the back seat of her own black Cadillac. Her
chauffeur drove her to the cemetery.

The graveside service was blessedly brief, though
it took a long time for the crowd to assemble around
the large green tent that sheltered the grave.

Reno's late mother, Sheila, shared the same head-
stone as Jess. Beau was buried next to his mother.
Caitlin's mother was buried in another section of the
cemetery, forever exiled.

The large number of mourners made Caitlin feel
self-conscious. She sat with Reno and Madison on the
chairs set out across from the casket for family, and
felt the curious stares of everyone near enough to see
her. When the brief service was over, she quietly got
to her feet, meaning to escape the ritual of greeting
the line of mourners who would file past the family
to extend final condolences.

She started to ease away from the chairs into the
crowd, but Reno stood and caught her elbow. His

touch was disturbing, and it shocked her when he started through the crowd, keeping her at his side. She heard a few murmurs of surprise, but the mourners parted before them in quiet deference.

Caitlin glanced once at Reno's iron profile, but his stern manner discouraged her from questioning his action. The driver of the funeral car opened the back door for them and Reno ushered her in.

The driver carefully pulled the car out of line to pass the parked hearse. Because there was no privacy window between them and the driver, neither of them spoke.

When they arrived back at the ranch, she and Reno got out of the car and walked into the house. Reno had hired extra help for Mary in anticipation of the crowd they expected after the funeral. The dining room table had been arranged for a buffet-style luncheon. Caitlin moved away from Reno to the front stairs.

"Where are you going?" The low question made her hesitate.

"I thought I'd go riding."

"We have company coming."

Caitlin gave her head a small shake, but didn't look back at him. "*You* have company coming."

She went tense waiting for Reno to demand that she stay.

"Take a cell phone."

His gruff order made her relax. She hadn't wanted to get into an argument with him, but she didn't want to stay at the house and endure the disapproval of the funeral guests.

It had already occurred to her that Reno had led her away from the graveside service to prevent that. His easy capitulation on the subject of her skipping the dinner and absenting herself from the house confirmed it.

Caitlin went quickly up the stairs. She changed her clothes and escaped to the range just as the first of the mourners arrived at the main house.

It was early evening when Caitlin arrived back at the stables. There was no activity at the main house. The cars that must have lined the driveway and parked on the lawn that afternoon were gone.

The moment she led her horse into the barn, she caught a whiff of sulphur and cigarette smoke. She dropped the gelding's reins, trusting him to stand, and walked quietly down the stable aisle to find the source of the odor.

Smoking in the stables and barns was forbidden with so much hay and wood around. Unable to find anyone in the barn, she walked back to the gelding. The smell of cigarette smoke still drifted in the air.

Childish voices from overhead made her glance up. The hayloft over the stable might not be full of hay this time of year, but it was still off-limits to smokers. From the sound of it, a couple of the children who lived with their families on the ranch were up there.

Caitlin walked to the ladder and quietly climbed up to the loft. Half the space under the large roof was packed with hay bales but, as she'd expected, the other half was empty except for some loose hay scattered on the plywood floor. A small fort of hay bales had been arranged near one side of the sloping roof. The giggles and kid voices—along with a haze of cigarette smoke—were coming from the hay fort.

She couldn't keep her boots perfectly silent on the plywood, and it squeaked beneath her feet as she crossed it.

Caitlin heard a gasp, then a wild shuffling. She reached the hay fort and looked over its low side just as the two boys were stubbing out the cigarette. The empty matchbooks and burned matches that littered the raw plywood between them told her this might not be the first time the two boys had hidden out in the loft playing with matches.

"Who are you?" Caitlin's voice was stern.

Both boys looked up, their dark eyes wide with surprise and fear. They couldn't have been older than nine or ten. It took them so long to answer that Caitlin repeated the question.

"That's Billy," the larger of the two said as he pointed to the other boy. "I'm Mike."

Caitlin dealt with them firmly, making them pick up every matchbook and matchstick, along with what was left of the cigarette. She checked the hay bales herself for any sign that a stray match or cigarette ash had fallen into them. While the boys stood by, she dismantled their hay fort and separated the bales. She escorted them down the ladder into the stable, then made them wait while she put up her horse.

Both boys seemed afraid of her and she did nothing to put them at ease. Better to make a scary impression on them now that would discourage further experimentation, than go easy on them and risk that they wouldn't take this seriously. Barn fires could be deadly, and she couldn't bear the thought of a child being caught in one.

She had them take her to their house. The cowhand who came to the door let them in. He called to his wife, who hurried in from the kitchen. The cowboy was initially respectful toward her, but Caitlin saw the wary disapproval in his dark gaze. His wife watched her with open suspicion.

Both parents stood by somberly as she showed them the mangled cigarette and blackened matches. When she finished the account, the cowboy's low "I'll deal with my boys, Miz Bodine," sounded more defensive than cooperative.

That both parents resented her was plain on their unsmiling faces. Nervousness made her try to placate them in some way.

"I remember when Lucky Reed caught me smoking in that same loft," she said, then offered the couple a slight smile to lighten their dark expressions. "It was…memorable."

Neither parent spoke. Instead, the wife's gaze sharpened on her as if she'd taken offense that Caitlin had compared anything about herself to her sons. Caitlin's slight smile faded.

Her soft "You have a pair of fine-looking boys," was not only a truthful observation, but one which she considered diplomatic. Unfortunately, it succeeded only in prolonging the hostile silence. Caitlin gave them a polite nod and turned to leave. The door banged closed behind her the moment she stepped outside.

Caitlin walked to the main house, shaken by the encounter. The barely concealed hostility of the cowboy and his wife was upsetting. Perhaps she should have told Reno about the boys and let him handle it.

By the time she reached the ranch house, Mary had finished working for the day. Caitlin could hear the TV on in Mary's quarters on the south wing of the main floor, so she helped herself to a few of the leftovers from the funeral dinner that day.

The ranch phone rang, but someone answered it on the second ring. Either Mary had picked it up or Reno had in the den, since he was probably doing paperwork.

She forced down a few bites of food, dismayed by her persistent lack of appetite, then gave up.

She went upstairs to get ready for bed. This was one day she was eager to put behind her. The funeral was over, and she'd gotten through it. She wanted to forget about the ranch hand and his wife, but the scene kept replaying in her mind. What did the other men on the Broken B really think of her? If she could inherit, would they ever accept her in any position of authority? What if they couldn't accept her presence on the ranch at all?

Once more she considered the wisdom of leaving it all behind, of leaving the Broken B forever. Suddenly it seemed she stood balanced precariously between a past she couldn't overcome and a future that would forever be hindered by the events of the past.

Restlessness made her finish her shower quickly and dry her hair. When she came out of the bathroom, the intercom on the night table was buzzing. Caitlin went directly to it and pressed the button.

Her "Yes?" was answered by Reno's brisk, "I want to see you right away." His voice was harsh and her unease multiplied.

Caitlin dressed in a clean pair of jeans and a blouse. She hurried down to the den, her stomach in knots. Something was wrong, and it didn't take a genius to figure out why Reno had suddenly ordered her downstairs. Her question about what the men on the Broken B thought of her was answered the moment she walked into the den.

"Dean Carnes and his wife are upset about you being around their boys."

Caitlin came forward, but didn't take a seat in one of the wing chairs. Reno was leaning back in the huge swivel chair behind the desk, his face harsh with disapproval.

"I caught the boys in the loft, smoking a cigarette and playing with matches."

Reno's dark brows lowered. He ignored her explanation. "They don't want you near their kids."

The statement made her heart sink. "If they'd started a fire in the loft, their parents might have something worse to worry about than me."

"Dean Carnes is more valuable to the ranch than you are right now, so stay away from them."

Stung, Caitlin's gaze wavered. "I'm certain you'd think a lame horse is more valuable to this ranch than I'll ever be," she said, then met his gaze squarely. "If I can inherit, Dean Carnes might have to be replaced."

"Carnes has a family to support," he pointed out grimly.

Caitlin nodded her agreement. "Maybe he'll need to keep that in mind."

Her implied threat charged the air between them. Reno gave her a look that glittered with temper.

"If you fire every man on this ranch who won't kiss your backside, we won't have enough men left to fill a pickup."

"They don't have to kiss my backside," she said quietly. "They only have to tolerate me and show reasonable respect."

"Respect is something you earn." Reno's low reminder hinted that respect was something she'd never have.

She lifted her chin. "The men will follow your lead."

The silence that followed her statement stretched out. Reno's harsh expression didn't change.

"Then give up."

Whatever small gain she thought she'd made with him evaporated. She swallowed hard at the emotions that were suddenly choking her. She struck back, but her voice was soft.

"Someday, you'll have to listen to what happened when Beau died."

Reno's glittering gaze dulled. "You were the reason Beau was at the canyon that day. If you hadn't gone off in a tantrum, he'd still be alive."

Though Reno's anger radiated toward her in hot waves, she stood her ground. When Reno's mother had become hysterical at the inquest and the judge had ordered her out of the courtroom, it had been Reno who'd escorted her out. ''You never did hear all of Lucky's testimony, none of Bob's or Tar's. And you never heard mine.''

Cold fury ignited in Reno's eyes before he broke contact with her steady gaze. He shoved his chair back and was on his feet so suddenly that the movement startled her. He reached for the scattered papers he'd been looking through and raked them into a rough pile. The repressed violence of his movements was telling. He didn't look at her again, though she could see a muscle in his jaw flexing wildly.

His growling ''Get out,'' was frightening.

Caitlin hesitated, but Reno was immovable. The frustration of it made her insides churn. The wall of hate between them seemed more formidable than ever. The dismal reminder that the truth—even if he knew it all—had the potential to make him hate her even more made her feel hopeless. She turned away and quietly left the room.

Her nightmare was as dark as the churning black water that thundered through the canyon and boiled against the ragged earth at its edge.

Caitlin was on her back, soaked and exhausted, gasping with terror and relief. Beau stood too near the edge of the canyon, and she told him so. Twice.

Suddenly, the earth trembled beneath her legs. Startled, she cried out as she sat up. Instinct made her scoot backward and hook a heel on solid ground. As the canyon side gave way, her foot slipped.

Beau's mocking smile switched to a look of surprise, then horror as the wide chunk of sod he'd been standing on fell away. Caitlin jerked her other leg back to catch her heel on solid ground the same instant Beau flung himself toward her. Time slowed to fractions of seconds as she saw Beau grab for her booted ankle and catch it. But she was yanking her foot backward in an instinctive scramble to save herself, and could only watch with shock-rounded eyes as Beau's hand slipped off the muddy leather...

Caitlin awoke to the sound of her own scream. Halfway out of bed and disoriented in the darkness, she stumbled and fell to her hands and knees. Icy chills quaked over her skin and she was so nauseated that she hung her head and panted sickly. Finally, she forced herself to her feet and staggered toward the bathroom.

Breathing carefully so she wouldn't be sick, she snapped on the light and moved to sit on the edge of the bathtub. The dream hadn't come this vividly in months.

You were the reason Beau was at the canyon that day...if you hadn't gone off in a tantrum, he'd still be alive.

Reno's words haunted her. He'd got it wrong, so wrong. She wasn't the reason Beau had been at the canyon, but in the end, she was the reason he'd died. She hadn't meant to kick his hand away. In saner moments, she knew he'd grabbed her boot at the wrong second and that her boot had been so slick with mud that he hadn't got a firm grip. Her other boot heel had already slipped off the sod and had crashed into water up to her knee. She couldn't have managed the leverage or time to try again before she fell in herself.

The bitter truth was that if she'd hesitated a fraction of a second, Beau might have had a chance. If she'd not instinctively yanked her foot back to catch her boot heel on solid ground, he might have been able to get a tighter grip on her ankle. Then he could have grabbed for the solid part of the bank with his other hand and got a firm hold before the water could tear him away.

But if she'd hesitated long enough for Beau to get a good grip on her boot, they both would have been swept away. That one small heel-hold ended up being the only thing that had saved her. Without it, she couldn't have moved backward far enough to keep from falling in with that part of the bank. As Beau had.

The hollow feeling of agony increased her nausea and she rested her temple wearily against the cool wall tile. Why had Beau been the one to die that day and she had not? Why couldn't she have died with him? However bleak and unhappy her life had been before that day, her life had ended when his had. However wild and cruel and selfish Beau'd been, he'd been loved and highly valued by everyone.

She sometimes wondered if that was part of the outrage over Beau's death. Outrage that the favorite had been taken away instead of the one who'd mattered so much less.

The heartbreak of it went over her in relentless waves of pain. She closed her eyes and made herself withstand it, though she didn't know why she bothered anymore. The memories never ended, never truly settled, and never allowed her peace. She'd coped with them at least well enough to function, but she was so tired of the battle, so tired of the failure.

Eventually, she made herself get up from the side of the bathtub and snap off the light. She walked through the dark to the bed and climbed in. Exhaustion eased her into sleep.

Jess's lawyer came to the ranch the next afternoon to read the will. As she'd suspected, Reno inherited everything—stocks, business holdings, gas and oil interests—and half the Broken B. She endured the lawyer's reading of the part about the blood test and felt again the cruel shock of it.

Suddenly she was struck by the realization that her father could have chosen something else to give her that would have been as valuable as half the ranch. Jess had other holdings of equal value he could have bequeathed to her, ones that would have freed her from a joint inheritance with Reno.

The fact that Jess had chosen to give her something that would put her at odds with the man who hated her was just another way of punishing her. And because she'd have to be Jess's biological daughter to be in the position to inherit jointly with Reno, it proved that blood really had nothing to do with her father's treatment of her.

The old insecurities stirred and swelled. The secret fear that she was unlovable was never more devastating than at that moment. Caitlin left the room the

instant the lawyer finished. Her copy of the will sat
on the desk, untouched.

The next few days were lonely and monotonous.
Caitlin had been away long enough to forget how
loneliness felt on the Broken B, but it wasn't long
until it struck her full force. Because Reno wanted
her to stay away from the men and not take part in
any of the work around the ranch, she had nothing to
do to pass the time. She took long rides during the
day, but it began to feel too much like her wanderings
through the big lonely ranch house in those two years
between her mother's death and her father's remar-
riage. The nightmares came every night now, and
without the distraction of work, they haunted her during the day.

Twice more, she'd looked through the house for
pictures of her mother, including her father's room in
the search, but she'd found nothing. She'd even called
Madison to ask her about them, but Maddie had refused to take her call.

Finally, four days after the funeral, Caitlin drove to
town and parked in front of the mansion that Madison
had inherited from their grandmother. She went up
the front walk and knocked on the door. A maid answered right away.

At her polite, "May I tell Miz St. John who's call-
in'?," Caitlin gave her name.

The maid's pleasant smile faded to a brittle line.
"Miz St. John isn't receivin' guests this afternoon,
Miz Bodine. Next time, please call before you drive
all the way into town."

The maid started to close the door, but Caitlin put up a hand to block it. "Would you mind giving her a message?"

Clearly the maid was wary of her, but she inclined her head politely to signal her agreement.

"I've been looking for pictures of my mother. I'd appreciate it if Miss St. John could find some for me. Our grandmother must have had at least a few."

"And where should Miz St. John call if she's able to find some?"

"I'll be at the ranch. If I'm not there, someone will know how to contact me."

The maid's brisk "Good afternoon," and her swift move to close the door left Caitlin standing awkwardly on the doorstep. She turned and walked back to her car.

Caitlin took a moment to glance at the huge homes that lined the other side of the street, their monstrous well-tended lawns separating each residence. The mansions on Madison's side of the street were just as large, the lawns just as spacious. Caitlin caught sight of two curtains—in the windows of two different houses—move, then swing back into place.

The idea that at least two people on the richest street in Coulter City felt compelled to keep an eye on her didn't improve her downcast mood.

By the next day, Caitlin had had enough. She had to have something to do. There were several solitary jobs on a ranch the size of the Broken B, so Reno would have to allow her to work. Because Jess had ordered the most definitive DNA test, it could be weeks before the results of the blood test were known.

Though she'd taken an indefinite leave of absence from her job in Montana, she'd go crazy if she didn't have anything productive to do with her time. At first, the chance that she couldn't inherit had made her want to stay and fight, or at least stay on in Texas for as long as she could, as a kind of farewell to the ranch she'd grown up on. Now she wasn't so sure the ranch or the wait was worth it.

She'd already decided not to contest the will if the blood test went against her. No sense impoverishing herself and wearing her heart out trying to get something no one wanted her to have. Even if the test results went her way, she wasn't certain how long she would stay. In a town the size of Coulter City and the surrounding ranch community, shunning was a very powerful and persuasive method of running off undesirables. If public attitude toward her—Reno's in particular—didn't change, she'd eventually have no choice but to leave the area.

In the meantime, she needed something to do. Every morning, Reno got up earlier than she did and had breakfast alone. He ate at the cookhouse at noon, then had Mary bring a supper tray to the den in the evening. Caitlin ate her meals in the dining room or on the patio out by the pool. Solitude hadn't improved her meager appetite.

The next morning, Caitlin was up at 4:00 a.m., twisting her long hair into a thick braid, then rushing silently down the back stairs to the kitchen. Because she'd reached the kitchen before Mary, she started a pot of coffee. Mary came in soon after, bid her a pleasant good morning, then efficiently began to cook breakfast.

Caitlin was sitting at the kitchen table with her shaking hands wrapped tightly around her coffee cup when she heard Reno's boot steps in the back hall.

That Reno wasn't pleased to see her up so early sitting at the table across from his chair was an understatement. Anger glinted in his eyes and his mouth settled into a flat line. Caitlin's nerves went raw with suspense. Mary was close enough to hear every word between them, and because the woman was the only person outside of Lucky, Tar and Bob who'd made her feel welcome, she was suddenly worried that Reno might say something hateful and change that.

Reno grabbed the first section of the newspaper and sat down. His gaze blazed into hers a few painful seconds before he glanced down at the paper, briefly scanned the front page, then briskly opened it.

Caitlin took a sip of hot coffee and felt her spirits sag lower. He hadn't said two words to her since that evening in the den when he'd ordered her out. Judging from his hard expression and the fact that he didn't look at her, he'd all but dismissed her from his part of the universe.

She glanced once at Mary, who was busily turning the pair of breakfast steaks under the broiler, then looked over at Reno. Her soft "I need a job to fill the time," was quiet, but determined.

Reno's gaze wavered on the newsprint he was reading, but he didn't glance her way, and his hard expression didn't change. "The employment office is downtown."

Caitlin labored to keep her voice steady and reasonable. "I saw the two-year-olds in the east pasture. I assume you had them moved there because you plan to have someone start handling them."

Reno turned a page of the paper. "Someone. *Not* you."

"There's tack in the stable that needs repair and clean—"

"Can't use you."

Reno didn't look up from the paper. Mary started their way with food. Reno heard her coming, then quickly folded the paper and laid it aside. Mary set two small serving platters between them, then turned and went for the others.

Caitlin watched Reno's hard features relax into a smile of thanks when Mary finished setting food before them. But the moment Mary walked away to unload the dishwasher from the night before, his smile vanished.

"I'm used to hard work," she told him under the cover of rattling silverware and dishes.

Reno's brisk movements as he cut into his steak hinted at temper. "How many times do you want to hear the word no?" His gaze came up and burned over her face.

Caitlin struggled to maintain eye contact with him. "I've heard the word all my life. If I let it stop me, I wouldn't be here now."

The quiet declaration made his face go rigid. His reaction—and the terrible meaning he took from her words—sent a wave of nausea over her. She'd meant it as an oblique reference to her father's refusal to love her, to allow her rightful place as his daughter, and all the important things that had been denied her as a result. That Reno connected her statement to his brother's death was horrifying. His low words confirmed it.

"Did Beau tell you no?" The demand came out in a growl. "Did he say it—did he *scream* it when you kicked him away?"

Caitlin felt the blood drain from her face. Reno thumped his knife and fork to the table. The sound made her jump. He stood up so abruptly that his chair clattered backward on two legs and teetered before it rooked forward and settled upright. He stalked from the table to the wall pegs, grabbed his hat, then slammed out the back door.

Caitlin stared down at her plate, stricken. She felt Mary's questioning gaze on her and struggled to behave normally. Reno had walked out on a full plate of food. She could hardly do the same, though she was certain she couldn't eat a bite.

Remembering what Reno had said the other night about Mary's feelings underscored his upset. If he could leave a full plate and risk hurting the cook's feelings, then he was violently upset.

Caitlin reluctantly picked up her fork and made herself eat.

CHAPTER FIVE

CAITLIN saddled the black gelding. She'd tried to stay at the house, but the huge rooms seemed so empty. Mary had politely declined her offer to help with housework. And because Mary was one of the few people who was pleasant to her, she'd not wanted to press. God knew how genuine Mary's pleasantness was, or how deep it went.

She hadn't seen much of Lucky or Bob or Tar these past days. When she'd caught sight of one of them, they were usually working with some of the other men, so she'd kept her distance. She had no wish to put any of them at odds with the men they had to work with.

Finished with the saddle, she swung up onto the gelding and rode down the alley that bisected the corrals. The thought of spending another day wandering the ranch depressed her. Perhaps tomorrow she'd drive to San Antonio. She'd already decided that spending time in Coulter City would lead to disaster. She'd considered finding some sort of work that needed to be done around the Broken B and just doing it, but it might be best to wait until Reno cooled off a little. If that was even possible.

Caitlin found herself riding toward the canyon. The dreams had been relentless. The longer she avoided that part of the ranch, the more intense they became.

Perhaps she'd been wrong to stay away. Perhaps there was some value to seeing it all again. Waking, she never allowed herself to remember all at once everything that had happened. The nightmares, however stark and realistic they were, rarely forced her to relive everything at one time either. But that might be because she was always able to fight them and bring herself to wakefulness before they could.

The moment she rode the gelding over the rise and saw the canyon, her heart began to beat heavily. The awful restlessness she'd been feeling twisted wildly inside her. She realized how tightly she held the reins when the gelding tossed his head and sidestepped to a nervous halt.

Forcing her grip to relax, she urged the horse down the hill and across the wide, dry grass verge that skirted the lip of the canyon. The gelding stopped several feet from the ragged edge.

Caitlin made herself dismount. She dropped the horse's reins, and while she worked up her courage, she stroked his glossy shoulder as he grazed.

It seemed to take forever to make her shaking legs carry her to the edge. The canyon was a wide, curving furrow that cut across a corner of Broken B land and eventually branched into two forks that went shallow about a half mile past the Broken B boundary. Easily one hundred feet wide here at the deepest bend of the creek, it was nearly thirty feet deep. The narrow creek at the base of the canyon was shallow enough to wade in this time of year and was maybe a dozen feet wide. To look at it now, it was hard to believe that the creek could ever flood so high that the canyon was filled and the waterline rose to within a foot of where she stood now.

A handful of horses grazed the tender green grass that grew on both sides of the creek at the bottom of the canyon. The sight was so peaceful and normal that the shock of that awful day struck her with fresh violence. Two colts near the creek nipped at each other, drawing her attention. When they began to frolic together, sharp images flashed in her mind....

A sorrel foal had been in the canyon that day. A few days old at the most, he'd blundered into the mud near the rain-swollen creek. Clumsy and easily spooked, he'd managed to mire his long legs deep in the mud. His black dam paced anxiously nearby.

Caitlin had heard the flash flood warnings earlier that day. Though it wasn't yet raining on the Broken B, she could see storm clouds several miles in the distance, and the dark gray sheet from cloud to ground that indicated torrential rains.

Filled with the foolish bravery and confidence of youth, she'd urged her horse onto the shallow path that angled down the wall of the canyon. The moment she reached the bottom, she shook out her rope and spurred her horse to the edge of the creek mud.

Once she had a loop on the foal, she dismounted and her horse stepped back to pull the rope taut. She worked her way down the rope, wading the sucking mud to half lift, half shove the foal out of the mire before she followed it out. She gently scolded the small, frightened animal and smoothly removed the rope. The mare rushed up to eagerly inspect her baby.

Caitlin could still recall her horror at the first trem-ors beneath her boots and the faint thunder of water up the canyon. The mare's head came up and she whickered nervously before she reached down to give her foal a sharp nip on the flank. The startled foal jumped forward and the mare bolted after her.

Caitlin's horse, the inexperienced three-year-old she'd been working with for the past few days, caught the mare's alarm and whirled to run with her, the rope still snubbed to his saddle horn.

The low thunder of water and the tremor beneath her feet increased the moment her horse took off. Caitlin glanced upstream, seeing the first rippling swell of water move around the curve and down the creek into her part of the long canyon.

The jolt of fear that went through her turned her knees to rubber. Flash floods were sudden and deadly. Terror made her break into a run for the canyon path. In the time it took her to reach the base of the path, the roar of water grew deafening. She raced up the path, stumbling once in her haste.

Halfway up, a rope fell over her head to her waist and cinched tightly. Startled, her arms trapped against her sides, she lost her balance and fell. She got her hands beneath her and jerked her head up, her atten-tion claimed by the huge wall of water that charged down the canyon toward her. Frantic, she slipped her arms free, but kept her unknown rescuer's loop around her waist as she scrambled to her feet and tried to reach the top of the path before the water struck.

She was within two feet of the goal when the wall of water knocked her off the path and slammed her

against the side of the canyon. Whoever held the rope
didn't let go. Dark water, gritty with dirt, filled her
mouth and nose and burned her eyes. Too disoriented
to do anything but cling to the rope and try to get a
breath of air, she felt herself being pulled steadily
upward.

Suddenly her head was above water and she was
clawing at the top of the bank. She was pulled
roughly over the edge and dragged several feet across
the grass before the rope abruptly went slack. Battered
and soaked, she lay helplessly on dry ground, coughing up the water she'd swallowed and sobbing wildly
for air.

"You owe me your hide, Little Britches."

Beau's boots stepped into her side vision and she
felt him loom over her. The sharp tug of the rope
reminded her it was still around her waist and that he
held the other end.

Another sharp tug and Beau's low "Might be a
good time to break you to ride," sent a fresh wave
of fear over her.

Beau's remarks to her lately had been crudely sexual. Jolted by his statement, she made an effort to get
to her feet. She managed to get to her hands and
knees, but Beau stepped back and yanked the rope to
make her fall flat. He dug the toe of his big boot into
her hip and forced her onto her back. Caitlin swung
her foot to kick him away, but he stepped between
her and the canyon to avoid it.

Using his superior strength, Beau kept the rope taut
to keep her on the ground....

*   *   *

The rattle of a bridle and the sound of a horse trotting down the hill behind her snapped Caitlin from the recollection. She glanced over her shoulder to see Reno pull his huge bay to a halt.

Though shaded by his hat brim, Reno's eyes were a fiery blue, and the silence between them was heavy with hate and disapproval. She got the impression that he considered her presence at the canyon to be a desecration of sorts.

Caitlin looked away from him and silently walked to her horse. She felt Reno's eyes on every move she made and was grateful when he didn't speak.

Remembering what had happened at breakfast and that Reno was predisposed to mistake anything she said to him, she said nothing either. The only sure way to deal with him was to keep silent. Once she was mounted, she glanced his way.

Apparently satisfied that she was leaving the canyon, his burning gaze made one brisk, dismissive sweep over her before he wheeled his horse and spurred it back the way he'd come.

Caitlin watched him go, her eyes tracing the strong, proud set of his wide shoulders. How many more ways could Reno demonstrate his loathing for her? She started the gelding in another direction. She couldn't live with Reno's hatred and hostile silences day in and day out for the rest of her life. She doubted she could tolerate them another day.

Caitlin rode back to the ranch headquarters late that afternoon. She put up the gelding, then walked to the house. Reno's bay was in his stall, so he was somewhere close by.

She'd decided to leave the ranch immediately. Reno had finally convinced her that they could never live together on the Broken B. Her experience with almost everyone else convinced her that she might never be able to live anywhere near this part of Texas. Waiting for the test results was a mere formality, since she no longer wanted the ranch.

But she was too restless to go back to Montana. The thought of waiting for the test results in town wasn't much more attractive. She'd go stir crazy at a motel and she wasn't up to facing the people there. Now even San Antonio seemed too close to the Broken B. Perhaps leaving Texas behind forever was the most healthy thing she could ever do.

She'd ridden out to the old homestead and spent a last hour there. As soon as she found Lucky and the others, she'd tell them goodbye. She'd stop at the cemetery in town to visit her mother's grave, maybe drive around Coulter City before dark to see what had changed and what was the same. Then she'd drive to San Antonio.

She debated the wisdom of trying one last time to talk to Reno about the day Beau died. The guilt she carried every waking hour made her ache for relief, however small. Though she hadn't deliberately killed Beau, she hadn't been able to save him either.

Confessing everything to Reno wouldn't guarantee that the burden would ease, wouldn't guarantee that he'd soften toward her, but the wild, secret hope that he might find some reason to forgive her never left her thoughts. The rational part of her brain reminded her that her account of that day might make things worse, so terror held her back.

On the other hand, now that she'd decided to leave the Broken B forever, what did she have to lose? She was giving up any claim to the Broken B anyway. Maybe she'd never go back to Montana, either. She didn't have a life there that was very valuable, since any wrangler could do the job she'd done on the SC. She had her inheritance from her grandmother, three aging cowhands who'd befriended her, but no one else who she'd allowed close. She'd already found out that she was hopeless with men, so she'd never have a family of her own. The future held nothing particularly attractive for her, and the knowledge made her feel reckless.

What was she really risking if Reno allowed her to tell him everything and things went badly? Was it possible to feel more guilt? Would her life really be so much worse if she threw away her last hope that Reno might change his mind about her? If life had taught her anything, it was that she could survive emotional trauma. The question was, did she really care anymore if she survived?

Weariness made her steps slow on the patio. She let herself in the back door and moved quietly through the hall to the stairs. Once she reached her room, she packed her things, then carried the suitcases down to her rental car.

Mary was nowhere around. Caitlin considered just leaving Reno a note. Thinking he was outside somewhere, she walked to the den for some paper.

* * *

Reno heard Caitlin come in and go upstairs. A part of him realized he'd overreacted that morning at breakfast, but damn her for the chaos she'd brought to his life. He'd been furious when he'd found her at the canyon. He didn't know how often she went there, and he suddenly didn't care.

He'd realized on his way back to the house that he hated the painful memories here. He'd decided to hand over every square inch of the Broken B to Caitlin, whether she was Jess Bodine's kid or not.

He'd give her everything else Jess had willed to him, too. He'd never wanted to inherit anything from Jess. He still had the Duvall Ranch near San Antonio. He'd added to it over the years, though it wasn't quite as large as the Broken B. For three years, he'd run this ranch for Jess, leaving his own ranch in the hands of his foreman. The two years before that, right after Beau died, he'd lived on the Broken B for long stretches because his mother's problems were so severe. After she'd died and Jess got sick, he'd moved to Coulter City for the duration. He'd missed being a daily part of his ranch, and as magnificent as the Broken B was, it had been too painful a place for him to get attached to.

He often wished his mother had never met Jess Bodine. And now that he was beginning to think less of Jess, he figured it was past time to go home and take care of what was his, time to find a wife and make his own family. He'd have the love of a good woman and the solace of home to heal him from the pain of the past five years.

The sound of Caitlin's footsteps in the hall made

him tense. Though he was giving her everything, he didn't want to see her, didn't want to have to speak to her or look at her beautiful face. He didn't want to see her tall, slender body and notice her lush curves or her beautiful mane of hair, didn't want to lust for her and be tormented by the knowledge that wanting her was disloyal to his dead brother.

He didn't look up when she walked through the open door.

Caitlin hesitated at the sight of Reno, then crossed the room to the desk. Without waiting for an invitation, she sat down on one of the wing chairs. He didn't look up and her heart sank. Now that she'd decided to try a last time to tell him about Beau, her insides were crawling with anxiety, and her mouth was so dry her tongue stuck to the roof of her mouth.

"I'm leaving the ranch."

She felt Reno's reaction, and waited only a second for his stormy gaze to streak up to hers. She almost couldn't go on. Her voice was soft, but she knew he could hear every word the moment she said, "I want to tell you about that day."

Reno's expression went black and she braced herself for his anger.

"My father lied about sending riders out to find me."

Reno got slowly to his feet, his face harsh with dislike. "Nothing you can say now will change anything. Beau will still be dead."

The words were brutal. Caitlin rose unsteadily to her feet as he came around the desk and strode to the door. *He was leaving the room.* Guilt knotted her throat, but she turned to follow him. "No one knows that better than me, but I need to—"

Reno turned on her then and seized her upper arms roughly. He gave her a slight shake. "You need to what?" he demanded, his hot breath gusting into her face. "Ease your conscience?" He practically sneered the words. "I don't want to hear anything you have to say, now or ever." He suddenly released her. "The ranch is yours. Everything Jess left is yours. You can have every acre, every holding, every damned dime of it and all the heartache and trouble it'll cause you. I'll take care of the lawyer and make sure it gets done legal, then I hope to God I never have to see your face again."

The cruel words made Caitlin shrink inside, made something in her heart wither and die. She felt so dizzy suddenly that she thought she would faint. Reno swung away from her and stalked from the room.

The air pounded in the aftermath of his rage. His words repeated in her mind, a harsh litany of hate that made it difficult to breathe, difficult to think.

Before she quite realized she'd taken a step, she found herself walking shakily out the back door. Her boots thudded dully on the patio stone as she walked to the part of the drive at the back of the large yard where she'd left her rental car.

She had to leave this place. Now. She didn't want the Broken B, she didn't want anything of Jess Bodine's. Reno's angry gesture did nothing but increase the terrible guilt she felt over Beau's death.

The shouts coming from the stable began to make an impression. Caitlin realized dazedly that black smoke was billowing out the loft door of the stable, and she began to notice that the smell of smoke was sharp in the air.

The scream of horses urged her toward the big barn, the frantic activity distracting her from her pain. She broke into a run.

The fire had burned through the big roof and licked wildly at the sky above it. Seconds later, the whole roof was ablaze. Men were running into the stable to lead frightened horses from their stalls.

A handful of wives and children stood well out of the way in a tight knot of worry as they watched more of the big barn catch fire. Two of the men aimed fire hoses at the flames, but the fire was too far along.

Caitlin stopped out of the way. One woman paced restlessly apart from the other wives, wringing her hands and glancing frantically around. The woman's obvious distress sent a tremor of foreboding through Caitlin as she recognized Mrs. Carnes, the mother of the two boys she'd caught smoking in the stable.

She rushed to the woman and caught her arm. "Where are your boys?"

The brimming eyes the woman turned on her were wild with fear. She shook her head. "I can't find them."

Caitlin glanced toward the barn. My God, *what if...*

Not consciously aware of the swift decision she made, Caitlin ran toward the doors of the stable. She dodged one of the horses that charged out of the smoky interior, but kept going. A cowhand material- ized out of the smoke, carrying one of the boys. She recognized him as the older one and rushed to the sobbing child.

"Where's your brother?"

The boy ignored her, but his hysterical sobs made her look toward the stable doors. The smoke was thick and now billowed so low that there was only two feet of clear air near the stable floor.

She heard the cowboy shout to the boy's mother, "What's he sayin'?", and felt such a staggering rush of fear that she was paralyzed. In one lightning moment of clarity, she understood what the boy had said. She could hear his sobs behind her and knew he was now crying too hard for his mother to understand.

Billy's still in there. Caitlin had heard the words clearly.

Two of the men staggered out of the smoke, dragging a third cowboy between them. The fire was hotter now and the smoke was so thick that it boiled in the stable aisle.

Billy's still in there.

If the boy had passed out from the heat and smoke, he might be lying somewhere inside. If he was flat on the ground, he might still be able to breathe. If he could breathe, he was still alive. Caitlin moved toward the stable numbly.

An eerie sense of destiny slipped over her. Her life wasn't worth much, so she was the logical choice to take the risk.

I hope to God I never have to see your face again. Reno's hateful words gave her a fatalistic calm and she broke into a run. Her last few breaths of good air were as deep as she could make them. She dimly heard the shouts of alarm as she plunged into the wall of smoke.

She ran blindly to the center of the stable and dropped to her hands and knees to escape the smoke, her eyes streaming. Her lungs were on fire from holding her breath and her first gasp of the air near the floor choked her. Narrow fingers of fire were cascading down to the tops of the stalls. The heat scorched her face and hands, and her clothes were painfully hot.

Caitlin felt her way along until she encountered the solid wall of the tack room just a few feet from the ladder to the loft. The fact that the door was shut was significant, since it was usually open. She'd heard that small children sometimes tried to hide from fires. Had Billy hidden in the tack room? It would be a stroke of good luck if he had.

The tack room door was solidly closed. Caitlin slid her hand up the heated wood for the door lever but discovered it was locked.

Coughing wildly in the smoke, she forced herself to her feet. If the door was locked without using the padlock on the outside of the door, then someone had locked it from the inside.

Dizzy from lack of oxygen, she kicked at the door. With every beat of her heart, she felt herself weaken, felt time running out. Giving one last effort, she kicked the door with all her might. The shock of pain that shot through her foot and radiated up her ankle told her she'd either sprained her foot or broken it.

The door gave way and she pushed it open. She dropped to her knees and bent low to swing her hands over the floor, searching for the boy. Her fingers encountered a small jeans-clad leg almost instantly.

The terrible coughing spasms that claimed her that same moment made lights flash behind her closed eyes. She was so weak now that she knew she could last only a few more moments. Struggling to stay conscious, she pulled the boy toward her, then backed out the door on her knees as she gathered his limp body close.

The roar of flames over the stable aisle was terrifying. She heard the warning groan of wood and got clumsily to her feet. The pain in her right foot made her stagger and limp, but she managed to stay on her feet and cling to the boy. The flames that licked down the stall fronts scorched her arms as she limped past. Dizziness made it difficult to navigate, and she could see nothing as she made the tortuous effort to escape. She guessed she was within only a few precious feet of the stable doors when she heard a loud whoosh.

A sudden burst of pain exploded like fireworks in her head, and sent her and the boy crashing to the stable floor.

Reno paced the waiting area outside the door that led to the emergency room. Billy Carnes was being treated for smoke inhalation. His terrified parents were with him, and his condition had stabilized. Though the boy was doing very well, they expected him to be admitted to the pediatric ward as soon as the staff could arrange it.

He didn't know about Caitlin. She had smoke inhalation, but she'd been burned when the loft floor beams had caved in on her. She'd sustained a head injury that had the potential to kill her all by itself.

No one had come out lately to give him a progress report, and it had been two hours since the last one. The fact that they were too busy with her to spare someone to bring him news seemed ominous.

Terror made him feel sick. His emotions were turbulent and wildly confused. The knowledge that he didn't want Caitlin to die—that he couldn't bear the thought—shocked him. It was a surprise to realize that as much as he'd hated her, he'd never for an instant wished her dead.

Her last words to him began another tortuous repeat in his mind. *I want to tell you about that day... My father lied...*

Somehow he cut the words off. But the moment he did, his last words to her pounded his conscience. *I hope to God I never have to see your face again...*

He'd meant every word when he'd said them. But now?

My father lied.

What had Jess lied about? The only thing he could think she was talking about was Jess's brief testimony at the inquest. Jess had said that Caitlin had worried everyone by haring off in a tantrum when there were flash-flood warnings out. After hours of worry, he and Beau and some of the men had gone out looking for her.

My father lied. The words made another track through his mind.

Caitlin had been raised on the Broken B. Whatever problems she'd had with jealousy and moodiness, or with Jess or Beau, she'd been as responsible and savvy and capable with the stock and ranch work as men who'd worked all their lives on ranches. He'd seen her in all kinds of weather, and he couldn't remember a time when she'd seemed reckless or foolish around potential danger.

Truth to tell, if anyone had been careless around the danger of flash floods, it was easier to believe it of Beau than of Caitlin. Jess had regularly berated Caitlin for even a hint of irresponsibility or incompetence, but he'd chuckled indulgently when Beau slipped up, and he'd bragged about Beau's nerve.

Beau, ever the daredevil, had constantly thumbed his nose at danger. He'd had too much crazy good luck to have learned any hard lessons, and that had made him more daring than ever.

Now Reno remembered the times when Jess had seemed to favor Beau over Caitlin. That was mainly the reason he'd gone out of his way to give her a bit of praise or a kind word when he was around. It had embarrassed him to see Beau get away with things that Caitlin could never think of doing.

The memory of Caitlin running into the burning stable sent a fresh shock over him. The Carnes had made their bad opinion of her clear, yet she'd charged in to save their kid as if they were her best friends. Clearly, she hadn't held their harsh attitude toward her against them. Had it been that way when Beau was killed? According to Lucky and the others, she'd been frantic to save him too.

Confusion cranked his turbulent emotions several notches higher. What the hell was going on in his head?

CHAPTER SIX

THEY moved Caitlin upstairs to the ICU late that night. The doctor was noncommittal about her chances. Her lungs were in better shape than any of the doctors had expected. Most of her burns weren't serious, but she'd be in pain for a while. When they couldn't remove her boot, they'd found out a bone in her right foot was broken. Her foot and ankle had been so swollen that they'd had to cut off the boot.

The worst injury was the concussion she'd sustained when she was hit by the falling debris. She hadn't regained consciousness.

When they let Reno into her ICU cubicle for a few moments, the sight of her pained him. Her face had been scorched by the terrible heat of the fire, and was shiny with the medication they'd put on it. Her eyebrows and eyelashes were singed, and her hair—which had been so glossy and magnificent and long—was now little more than shoulder length. The nurses had cut off the rest, but a hairdresser would have to do a better job later.

Her hands and arms were lightly bandaged, and he could see the bulk of heavier bandages on her left shoulder under her hospital gown. Her right foot and ankle had been carefully propped up on pillows, but didn't have a cast yet.

Reno stood at her bedside and stared grimly,

watching as she coughed weakly in her sleep. The compulsion to touch her, maybe speak to her, made him grip the bed rail and grit his teeth. She didn't have anyone who cared for her except Lucky, Bob and Tar. But none of them were family, so none of them were allowed into the ICU. He'd called Madison St. John, but she was in New York.

He didn't realize he'd reached for Caitlin until his fingers brushed the bandages on her arm. What was this peculiar sympathy he felt for her? Why was the strange connection he felt to her so deep and so compelling?

There was no way to account for the tenderness he felt now. God help him, what if he'd been wrong about her?

After a few moments of indecision, he reached to touch her hair. Her head was literally the only appropriate place he might safely touch her without causing her pain. He fingered a lock, then lightly smoothed her hair back from her shiny forehead.

The faint flicker of her eyelids and the slight move of her head made him pause. But when he stroked her gently a second time, there was no response.

"Get well, Caitlin Bodine," he whispered gruffly. Something harsh and unforgiving in his heart finally relented. "Get well, then tell me about that day."

He lingered until the nurse stepped in and made him leave.

The next afternoon, Reno came home from the hospital for a shower and fresh clothes. He took care of a little book work while he was there, but he was in a hurry to get back to the ICU. Lucky Reed caught him in the den as he was finishing up.

"How's Miz Caitlin?" The old cowhand's weathered face was lined with concern. Reno had called him last night and again that morning, but that was hours ago now.

Reno motioned for him to sit and Lucky eased himself onto one of the wing chairs. "Still unconscious when I left. The hospital hasn't called with any change, so she must be the same."

Lucky gave him a searching look. "You gonna spend time up there with her?" As if he realized the question was forward, he added, "You bein' the only close family she's got left." The statement told Reno what Lucky expected of Madison St. John.

"Unless her cousin comes back early from New York." Reno watched the old cowboy. He knew what was coming. He could tell by the determined glint in the old man's eyes. Lucky glanced down at the floor for several moments as if collecting his thoughts, and Reno waited until Lucky's gaze came up to his.

"When Miz Caitlin was gone, there wasn't much point in tryin' to talk to you. You never seemed inclined to hear the whole story, and Jess would never've let her come home anyway." He looked down to pinch the crease of the battered hat he held in his work-scarred hands. "She's been back long enough for the two of you to settle your differences," he said, then looked up again. "Have you?"

Reno didn't take offense at the question, though they both knew Lucky was out of line. "We've got more than differences between us."

Lucky shook his head. "You can fire me if you like, Boss, but if the two of you ain't settled things, then I gotta speak up."

Suddenly restless, Reno leaned back in the swivel chair and rested his elbows on the chair arms. He respected the man's age and good character too much to refuse to hear him out. "I heard your testimony."

"Yep, you did. But you didn't hear the whole of it. I don't reckon ol' Jess woulda told you anything, if he could even tell the truth anymore."

Reno's gaze narrowed on the cowhand's face. "Are you saying Jess lied?"

Lucky gave a nod. "Yessir, I am. Besides bein' a spiteful man, he lied at the inquest about worryin' over Miz Caitlin and goin' out to search. Weren't nobody out lookin' for her. On top of which, there weren't much Jess ever told about that girl that was the whole truth." He shook his head. "Never made sense how he treated her, but he's dead now. I figger it's left to the livin' to make things right."

The solemn pronouncement was the lead-in to a recitation of what Lucky had seen of Jess's relationship with his only child. As Reno had begun to suspect, Jess had been anything but loving and kind to his daughter.

Lucky moved into his account of what he'd seen at the canyon. But before he was halfway through, something he said—or rather something he left out—made Reno interrupt.

"If Caitlin and Beau were both at the edge of the canyon and you could see that they both looked safe, why were you riding hell for leather to get to them?"

Reno had never understood that part of what he knew, and now he wanted an answer.

Lucky's sudden reluctance to answer was plain in the way his gaze shifted from Reno's. He looked uncomfortable.

"Someone dies, it's best to remember the good about 'em."

Everything in Reno came to full alert and he felt queasy suddenly. "Don't speak ill of the dead?"

Lucky didn't look at him straight on. "That's right. Not no point. The loved ones left behind got enough pain to face when someone that young gits killed. No sense puttin' burdens on 'em that can jest as well go by."

Lucky fingered his hat brim again in the waiting silence before he went on.

"I reckon we took the wrong course. Didn't seem like the whole story needed to be told for the judge, since he was mainly interested in did she kill him or not." Lucky's eyes came up to his. "If we'd a-knowed how it would go for Miz Caitlin after, with you hatin' her and Jess runnin' her off, we woulda told it all then."

The level look the old man gave him was solemn and deeply convincing. Reno stared back, his insides a maelstrom of volatile emotions. His voice was hoarse with them.

"Maybe you ought to tell it all now." The moment he said the words, a sick feeling of intuition quivered over him. He knew instantly he would hear the truth.

Lucky's somber eyes showed a flicker of sympathy. "Then you need to know that Beau pulled Caitlin outta the water. He saved her life by throwin' a rope on her and pullin' her up. We didn't see that part, but it was in Miz Caitlin's testimony. When we saw them, she was on the bank with his rope on her, but he wasn't takin' it off and he wasn't lettin' her get on her feet.

"I'd heard some of the things he'd been sayin' to her lately when he thought nobody was around. Remarks a gentleman ought not make to a female."

Lucky stopped to let his words sink in, but he was watching Reno's grim face closely.

"Go on."

The old man's reluctance showed in the way he hesitated over his next words.

"Looked to me like he was goin' to force himself on her. Don't know how much he had in mind or if he was just teasin' her again, but ever' time she tried to get up, he'd use the rope to keep her down. That's when we started ridin' for the canyon." Lucky's discomfort was acute and he was pinching the crease of his hat mercilessly.

"While he was doin' that, he was backin' toward the water like he was thinkin' of tossin' her back in. Once, he took hold of her boot like he was gonna drag her to it, but he let go. Then he went over to walk along the edge of the canyon, balancin' himself like he was on a tightrope." Lucky paused.

"That was when the bank caved in. She was tryin' to shove herself back 'cause there wasn't much ground left under her legs, and Beau threw himself to grab onto her. He musta let go of the rope then."

There was silence again as the old man waited for

him to take it in. Reno's heart was heavy with grief, but his question carried a trace of defiance. "Did she kick him into the water?"

Lucky's gaze didn't waver from his. "No, sir, she didn't, not on purpose. Was a case of her makin' a natural move back and him grabbin' for her while she was movin'. Because they was right on the bend of the canyon where the water hit hardest, it took him at the same split second so he never coulda held on. Likely, he woulda pulled her in with him. Even if he'd still had a-hold of that rope he had on her, I don't know that she coulda kept either one of them out of the water."

Reno looked down at the desk, numbed by it all, reliving the pain of Beau's death, but with the added knowledge that Beau's foolish antics on the very brink of the flooded canyon had caused his own death. And what had he meant to do to Caitlin? The answer shamed him.

"And Caitlin tried to save him." It was a statement, but Lucky answered.

"Never seen anyone try harder. If we hadn't of got there, she'd of kept tryin' till she died with him. Her goin' in the fire after that boy proves the stuff she's made of."

Lucky paused several moments. Reno struggled with his thoughts and with the sharp guilt that slowly pounded deep into his chest. The guilt switched to agony when Lucky went on quietly.

"Never heard a human bein' make the kind of grief sound that girl made when we held her back from goin' in after him. Was more like somethin' wild was havin' its heart tore out than a person. Much as she had against your brother, when it come down to it, none of it mattered.''

Reno's breath squeezed out of him in a spasm of pain so strong it made his eyes burn. His low ''You've had your say,'' was as much as he was capable of.

He was reeling with the shock of it all. There was no question in his mind, everything Lucky had told him was the truth. And not just because Lucky was credible, but because somewhere in his heart he knew the old man's account fit what he knew about Caitlin's character and his brother's.

The bitter memory of the hateful things he'd said to Caitlin, everything he'd done, knotted his gut. Lucky's gruff question tortured him.

''Do the doctors think she'll pull through?''

Reno swiveled his chair slightly away from the old man. The evasive move was uncommon for him, but his conscience was pounding him and it was hard to speak. ''The head injury is the biggest problem. The sooner she wakes up the better. They're…cautious.''

He was so focused on his thoughts, so preoccupied with what Lucky had told him and the guilty knowledge that his hatred had brutalized Caitlin, that he wasn't aware when Lucky got up and quietly left the room.

Caitlin was first aware of the pain. Her head pulsed with it. She tried to lift her hand in an instinctive move to soothe it, but the movement sent fire from her shoulder to her fingertips. Suddenly her whole body hurt and she wasn't coherent enough to understand why. The faint sound of distress she heard was hoarse and it made her throat hurt. It was with some surprise that she realized the painful sound was coming out of her.

"Caitlin Bodine?"

The firm male voice got her attention and she tried to turn her face toward it. Bright sparks of agony streaked behind her closed eyelids, startling a gasp out of her that made her throat ache harder. A brief coughing spasm tore at her throat and chest, and the pain in her head was excruciating. It took a few moments of utter stillness to calm the pain.

Her softly croaking "Hurts," was all she could manage.

"Okay, Caitlin, we'll take care of it."

In seconds, she felt something spread through her that soothed the sharp edges of the pain and sent it away.

A day later, a voice woke her. She carefully opened her eyes, defying the bright lights that made the task so painful. A shadow loomed over the side of the bed and she blinked to focus on it.

"Are you awake?" The low words were gruff, and she instantly recognized Reno's voice. Joy sang through her those first seconds until memory snuffed it out.

Fire. There'd been a fire. And something else…the boy. She remembered the dangerous, terrifying search.

"The boy—is he...alive?" She ignored the strange rasp of her voice in her anxiety to have an answer.

"The boy's fine. Home with his family."

Her relief was profound, and she was suddenly too weary to keep her eyes open. The blurriness was too much to overcome.

Reno's words "Thanks to you, he's alive," sent a tiny shaft of pleasure through her, but another memory made it freeze in her heart.

I hope to God I never have to see your face again.

The ache in her chest throbbed into her throat and made her head pound. She couldn't take anymore, couldn't bear to hear another hateful word. Her labored "Get away from me," was little more than a pained whisper. She felt Reno lean closer.

"It's all right, baby."

The soothing words made it difficult to resist the craving for more that burst up and filled her heart with hope.

But she'd never crave love again, she'd never hope for anything good to come her way. She'd lived twenty-three years on hunger and hope, but she was so weary of failure that she wouldn't waste another second on either of those things.

She gritted her teeth against the agony in her heart. "I said, *get away from me.*"

She felt Reno's shock before a new voice intruded.

"I'm sorry, Mr. Duvall. Perhaps you can come back later."

Caitlin heard. Her eyelids were burning and her throat felt raw as she got out, "No. Don't come back."

Agitation made her restless, but every small move she made hurt.

"I'm sorry, Mr. Duvall, you'll have to leave."

A cool, unfamiliar hand touched her forehead and she sensed that the hand and the voice belonged to the person who'd suddenly stepped between her and Reno.

His low "I'll be back," was a vow.

Caitlin felt herself weaken. The moisture that soothed her burning eyelids streaked from the corners of her eyes into her hair as she heard his boot steps recede. She was too miserable to be relieved.

She'd managed to make it clear to the nurses that she didn't want Reno Duvall allowed in the ICU. If they were curious about that, they kept it to themselves. But then, Caitlin had been too weak to be aware of much because she'd slept every moment that their nursing schedule allowed. In another four days, Caitlin was moved to a private room on another floor.

Though she didn't seriously think anyone except Lucky and the others would care to visit her, she'd requested that no visitors be allowed into her private room, and that no one be given her room number. Nevertheless, get-well flower bouquets began to arrive. First from Reno, then one from Lucky, Bob and Tar, then one from Billy's family. She called the ranch right away to speak to Lucky and thank him and the others for the flowers they'd sent, then followed up the call with a personal note to each of the three men. She sent a brief note of thanks to the Carnes, but she tried to ignore the roses Reno sent.

She didn't understand the gesture from him and tried not to think about it.

Now that she was in a private room, she was allowed to sleep longer without interruption, and the constant fatigue that plagued her made avoiding sleep impossible. After two more days, some of her lighter bandages came off. She was able to walk short distances on the walking cast, but she tired in a frustratingly short period of time.

Her hair had been burned. She'd cried when she'd realized it, then felt foolish because it was such a minor loss. Both she and the boy could have died. But the minor burns on her skin were far less upsetting to her than the damage to her hair.

The soothing ointment they used on her scorched face was rapidly healing the skin there, and she'd have no burn scars on her face, arms or hands. Only a tiny part of the burns on her shoulder and back were second degree, and no one would ever see those scars.

Her vision had cleared, but she was plagued by headaches that grew worse when she was tired. Because she had no one to take care of her, the doctors were reluctant to approve her release from the hospital.

She tried not to think about Reno. Why had he come to the hospital? Why had he spoken so gently to her? Why had he sent the roses? The questions hounded her, and though the strain of not thinking about them wore her out, she made the effort.

Because she'd finally gotten smart. Love and family were not possible for some people, certainly not for her. She'd never open her heart to that kind of pain again. She couldn't let herself hope that Reno might finally have softened toward her, when his actions were probably motivated by simple pity for her injuries. Besides, she'd never again try to tell him about Beau, so it didn't matter why he was doing these confusing things now.

After she left the hospital, maybe she'd live like Maddie did. She'd buy herself a grand house somewhere where no one knew her, or a small ranch, and live as she pleased, investing her money, living her life as a rich hermit who needed no one. She'd never been out of the country, so maybe she could travel. Perhaps she could find a charity and throw herself into that. As long as she didn't interact with anyone on a personal basis...

Reno had given Caitlin time to get better. He'd given her eight days.

He'd managed to track her progress through a woman on the hospital housekeeping staff who was married to one of his men. While he hadn't asked her to snoop in Caitlin's medical chart, she'd been able to tell him how Caitlin looked, whether she was able to get out of bed and move around, and how well she seemed to feel.

He'd waited every day for a new report, but was frustrated when the woman had a day off and nothing new to tell. Time crawled even slower on those days, and his impatience to see Caitlin climbed to monstrous proportions.

After eight days, he'd reached his limit. He'd see her tomorrow, whether she wanted to see him or not.

He'd done her a grave injustice, they all had. But the injustice he'd done to her was so large and so terrible that letting her have her wish to keep him away would only compound it. She needed to know that things had changed, she deserved to know that he no longer blamed her, that he was sorry and meant to make it up to her.

And now that he knew everything about Beau's death, the attraction he felt toward Caitlin had become deeper and more profound.

He'd talk to her doctor first thing in the morning.

Caitlin returned wearily to her room after her first major walk without the encumbrance of the IV stand. The doctors had tentatively agreed to release her later that morning, so the IV had been taken out. Because she knew they might not approve her release if they knew she planned to spend a few days at a motel until she felt like driving to San Antonio, she'd been vague about where she would be going when they let her out.

She'd called the ranch and asked that her rental car and her belongings be brought to the hospital. She'd asked Lucky to bring them because she was eager to see the old cowhand. She hoped he hadn't been offended by her request for no visitors. When she'd spoken to him on the phone about the flowers a few days ago, he'd seemed to understand. But then, Lucky was too kind and too much a gentleman to ever let her know if he'd taken offense, so she'd worried about it.

Regret made her sigh as she set her cane aside and

climbed gingerly onto the bed. She lay back and pulled the sheet and light blanket over herself. God, she hated regret. Was there anything she would ever do right? She closed her eyes and tried to banish the feeling. Regret and guilt couldn't be part of the new life she was going to make for herself. She'd had enough of guilt and enough regrets to last two lifetimes.

Her head was throbbing again, but she resisted the urge to ask for more medication. She was exhausted enough after her walk to fall asleep without it.

The sound of the door swishing open woke her later. She forced away the lingering fog and glanced toward the sound. She'd expected Lucky to bring her things sometime that morning so she could get dressed, but the cowboy who walked into the room was Reno.

Her first unwary glimpse of him sent a bolt of excitement through her. She stared, hardly believing her eyes as she watched him cross to her bed and set her overnight bag beside the nightstand.

The next moment her excitement switched to panic. She reached for the call button fastened to the bed sheet beside her, but Reno's hand shot out to unclip it and snatch it away. He set it out of reach on the nightstand.

"We need to talk." Reno's tone was no-nonsense.

Her instant "I've got nothing to say to you," made his stern expression harden. She found the button to raise the head of the bed. He allowed her to raise it to a sitting position before he leaned down to brace his fists on the mattress on either side of her thighs and loom close.

"That's good. I'll do all the talking." He didn't give her time to object. "I'm taking you home. I'll hire a nurse if you need one, but you'll be well taken care of. When you feel up to it, you can decide what you want to do with the ranch. It's yours. You can run it yourself, have someone run it for you, or sell it off. You're a respected member of the community, so you'll be able to choose anything you damned well please."

Caitlin's heart caught on the words *You're a respected member of the community*. Her eyes stung with pain.

"Since when?"

The flicker of softness in Reno's eyes had to be her imagination going wild. His voice went low.

"By now, everyone knows what happened when Beau died. And risking your life to save the boy has made you a heroine."

Caitlin almost couldn't choke back her emotions. "So, even though I murdered Beau, saving the boy makes up for it? A one-for-two record is nothing to brag about."

Reno shifted. His hand caught hers gently.

"Everyone knows what happened when Beau died. They know he put his own life in danger, that you aren't responsible for his death in any way."

Caitlin's breath caught. Surely she was imagining this. Five years of pain made itself felt, five years of lonely, guilt-ridden exile. The faces of everyone at the funeral, Maddie, the cowboy and his wife—

Reno—flashed in her mind. The harsh, unfriendly faces, the self-righteous, condemning faces of the people who'd considered her a murderess. She couldn't accept—or trust in—this sudden reversal.

Caitlin threw off his hand. "Get out."

The faint glint of shock in his eyes was the only chink in his take-charge armor.

"I'm here to take you home where you belong."

"I don't have a home," she insisted bitterly.

"You do now."

The calm words stoked her fury. "Surely you don't go along with all this. It was your brother I killed."

"You didn't kill Beau."

The words she'd hoped to hear, the words she would have accepted if he'd ever allowed her to tell him what happened, sent a flash fire of resentment through her.

Her angry "How do you know?" made her voice tremble.

"Lucky and I had a talk," he said gruffly. "I know what happened at the canyon." He paused and she had to glance away from the regret in his eyes. "I know I can't ever—"

"What?" The remark brought her gaze back to his and she flashed him an angry look. "You couldn't bear to listen to me, but you and Lucky have a talk and suddenly you know everything? You *believe* everything?" Her voice rose with each word. She shook her head and looked away.

She'd tried to tell him herself, but he'd hated her too much to listen. She'd lived in agony these past years, lived with crippling guilt and the pain of

Reno's hatred. Then the fire had broken out. If it hadn't, she'd be long gone by now and none of this would be happening. But because she'd saved the boy and been injured, suddenly Reno was willing to listen to the truth.

If there had been no fire, Reno would have gone on blaming her—and hating her—for the rest of his life.

"I came here to apologize."

Her gaze flew to his and his solemn look made her boil. She was so furious she could barely speak.

"Lucky says a few words, you suddenly believe him, so now everything is wonderful, all's forgiven, let's be friends?"

Her belligerence clearly surprised him and she gave a bitter chuckle. "Thanks for the offer of an apology, Reno, but no thanks. Lucky might not be there the next time my word or actions are called into question." She sat up straighter to emphasize her words.

"There's no way I'll ever live someplace where people rush to believe the worst of me, where no one believes anything I say. And if you'll recall, Lucky and the others' testimony *and* a judge's ruling weren't enough to back me up the first time around. Now suddenly, because I tried to save a child from a fire, what Lucky has to say about me is gospel? *Oh, no thanks.*"

Caitlin shook her head adamantly, then flinched at the pain in her head and reached up briefly to soothe it. She was beyond upset. She was so angry, so furious that she couldn't contain herself.

As if concerned by the gesture that signaled pain,

Reno touched her, but the jolt of awareness that went through her set her off again. She lifted her hands to Reno's chest to press him back. The effort barely moved him, but he moved back to appease her.

"No one in their right mind would live in a place where people make such harsh judgments," she railed, "then, over some minor act of heroism, make such sweeping reversals."

Her eyes were blazing and she was shaking wildly. "What happens during the next flood or barn fire? If I can't save the next one, will everyone's opinion swing back the other way?"

Outrage and pain set off a new geyser of emotion. Her eyes were stinging, but she fought the urge to cry. She'd die before she gave in to the overwhelming urge to sob out her disappointment in the reason for everyone's change of heart.

She couldn't help that her voice was choked. "And you're the worst of all," she declared hoarsely. She had to turn her face away before she shamed herself. Her head was pounding so hard she was nauseous.

Suddenly, her doctor strode into the room and Caitlin was pitifully grateful for the interruption that kept either of them from saying more.

"Is everything okay?"

Caitlin gritted her teeth and made one small, stiff nod. She forced herself to look at the doctor and give him a tight smile to prove it.

"Mr. Duvall assures us that you'll be well taken care of at home."

Caitlin's angry gaze shot to Reno's and glowed resentfully. "I can take care of myself. I'm going to a motel."

The doctor's pleasant smile faded to a sober line. "If that's the case, we may have to keep you longer. You shouldn't be alone until you've recovered a bit more from that concussion." He paused and his gaze searched hers. "Right now, my guess is your head's pounding like a bass drum."

Tears stung her eyes at his perception. Her head hurt terribly. Her whole body ached and she was weak. Rage had drained her and she doubted she had the strength to get out of bed.

"I'm tired of being here." The admission was difficult to make without sounding as weak and weepy as she felt.

The doctor nodded. "Then why don't you let Mr. Duvall take you home? He explained the situation to me, and I have his assurance that you'll be very comfortable and happy in your home."

The gentle words were persuasive. Caitlin saw the quick look that flashed between the two men. It was a confirmation that they'd conspired together against her.

"H-how long before I can reasonably take care of myself?"

The doctor looked relieved, and so did Reno. "A couple of weeks will make a huge difference. We'll take off the shoulder bandage now, and switch the hard cast for a removable one with Velcro straps. As I said, the concussion is the thing we want to watch. You can walk on the foot, but doing everything for yourself is still too much. You need good food, plenty of rest and more time.''

Caitlin felt herself losing the battle. But once she was on the Broken B and no one was watching, she could leave. The doctor was exaggerating. She wasn't helpless. She was weak and uncomfortable, but she could cope on her own. She didn't need anyone, least of all Reno Duvall.

She made herself give a small nod of agreement, then submitted to a final exam after Reno stepped out of the room.

She'd go with him now to the ranch. But she'd leave on her own at the first opportunity.

CHAPTER SEVEN

HE'D been arrogant to think he could waltz into Caitlin's room, apologize, and that it would be enough. He'd been hard on her, too damned hard, and he couldn't blame her for blowing up at him. He'd put her through too much, hurt her too much for her to get over it easily.

In spite of her towering anger just now, Caitlin had been in terrible emotional pain. He'd seen it, but he'd also seen her fear. She was terrified of everyone's change of heart, and when he thought about it from her side, he could understand.

Like she'd said, she'd told the truth at the inquest and had testimony that backed hers up. The judge had ruled that she wasn't responsible for Beau's death, but everyone else had judged her guilty. Especially him. Now everything had changed, and she was afraid it could just as easily change again.

Was it even possible for her to forgive him? Until Lucky had gotten through to him, it might never have been possible for Reno to forgive her.

But this was about much more than Caitlin forgiving him for what he'd done to her. It was about him making things right, about restoring what she'd lost, and maybe giving her the things she'd never had. Caitlin was still that lonely, heartbroken kid who hadn't been loved or treated very well by the important people in her life, him included.

He remembered even more clearly now when she was a kid. Though she'd tried to hide it behind her solemn glances and carefully neutral expressions, he'd seen her excitement when he came around. A word of praise, no matter how minor, sent a blushing glow to her pretty face that she'd immediately tried to conceal. Sometimes, as if his praise was too wonderful for her to stand, she'd become even more shy and find some excuse to get away from him for a while. The sad part was that he'd never said anything particularly lavish to her. Just a couple of laconic words now and then.

He'd sensed right off that she was starved for attention, and once he'd given her a little, she'd shadowed his every move in hope of more. But as she got older, he'd become uneasy with that. He was ten years older than she was, so when those solemn blue eyes began to show hints of infatuation, he'd distanced himself from her.

He knew he'd hurt her then, but there'd been no help for it. A teenaged girl had no business developing a crush on a man who was ten years older, and a decent man would never encourage it.

But now that Caitlin was a mature twenty-three, the ten-year age difference between them didn't matter. At least not to him.

The doctor came out of the room then, and gave him a nod. He explained some of the limitations he wanted Caitlin to keep and when he wanted to see her in his office. After the doctor left, Reno turned toward her room and prepared himself for her resistance.

Caitlin fought him. Though he could see she was worn out, he'd asked her if she'd like to stop by a beauty shop to have her hair trimmed. It didn't look that bad to him, but he'd seen her catch sight of her reflection in the plate glass in the front lobby of the hospital. She'd lifted a hand and touched one of the jagged locks, and he'd sensed then that she was self-conscious about the way it looked.

Once she was in the car and the overnight bag he'd brought was stowed in the trunk, she'd not looked his way. His offer to stop by the salon had made her stiffen, but she'd nodded. Once they arrived at one of the better ones in Coulter City, she'd refused to let him help her to the door. Even with the cane she'd brought from the hospital her progress was slow, and by the time she reached the door of the salon, he could see the perspiration that had broken out on her face. The sun was hot, and the tender exposed skin of her face and hands must have been smarting, but she'd gritted her teeth and endured it.

Once inside, she was instantly recognized. The women in the place tracked her every move. The stylist—who was also the owner of the shop—took care of her, first shampooing her hair, then giving it a good cut with a couple of subtle layers that trimmed the damaged parts away and restored a healthy look. Caitlin declined to have her hair dried, and Reno knew it was as much because she was too worn out to wait as it was because the air from the dryer would be too hot for her skin.

Caitlin looked profoundly uncomfortable when the owner refused her money and cheerfully told her that the shampoo and cut were on the house. Her declaration that she was proud to have Caitlin Bodine come to her shop, sent a tide of fiery color up Caitlin's cheeks. Though she thanked the woman, by the time they got to the car, Reno could see she was shaking with embarrassment and fatigue.

Once Reno was in the car and got it started, his quiet "Things have changed for you," sent her temper skyward.

"Today they're changed," she burst out. "Tomorrow they can change again." She glanced his way then, and he saw the fear in her eyes. He reached to touch her, but she shifted her arm to avoid him.

"Anywhere else you'd like to go?"

Caitlin gave her head a small shake and faced forward, drawing into herself as if she were under attack.

Five minutes later, her head eased back on the headrest. Reno glanced her way and saw that she was deeply asleep. Exhaustion left gray smudges under her eyes. She had no stamina and no real strength. The doctor had said it would be some time before she fully recovered, and from the look of her now, Reno believed it. She'd been going on anger and willpower since he'd got to her room that morning and upset her.

She didn't wake up when they reached the ranch and he parked the car along the part of the driveway nearest the house. She was so deeply asleep that she didn't know when he opened her door, touched her seat belt release and carefully gathered her limp body into his arms.

Taking care not to jostle her or to carry her in a way that might put pressure where she'd been burned, he eased her cheek against his shoulder and slowly lifted her out of the car. He carried her across the back patio past the pool and went into the door that Mary held open for him.

Reno carried her through the house and up the stairs to her room. Mary had already turned down the sheet and bedspread, so he laid Caitlin down gently. He carefully pulled off her left boot, then reached for the small stack of pillows Mary had set out on a nearby chair. He propped up the Velcro cast, then pulled the sheet and bedspread up to her chin.

He looked down at her a moment, then reached to pluck a lock of dark hair that had fallen over her cheek and move it aside. He touched her skin lightly with the back of a finger.

Before he left the room, he switched on the intercom on the night table. If she needed anything, he wanted to know it immediately. On his way out, he glanced back, struck again by how weak she looked now, how frail. When she woke up, they'd discuss hiring that nurse.

Caitlin woke up late that afternoon. A few minutes after she limped to the bathroom to freshen up then returned to sit on the side of her bed, Reno was knocking on her bedroom door.

His low voice carried from the hall. "I can take you downstairs if you're ready."

Caitlin was uneasy with the offer. It had been disorienting to wake up in her bed at the ranch, her boot off and her other foot propped carefully on pillows. She had no memory of arriving at the ranch and no memory of being carried upstairs and put to bed. Because Reno must have done it, she felt self-conscious and exposed. And vulnerable.

Reno had changed toward her. Dramatically. And the change in him terrified her.

Now she remembered the charge that had gone through her at the hospital. There'd been something intense and sexual about the way he'd braced his fists beside her on the bed and leaned down into her face.

He'd been so close that she'd seen every fleck of navy in his blue eyes and every dark hair on his hard jaw. Though he'd shaved that morning, she'd seen the hint of heavy beard that shadowed his ruggedly handsome features. The smell of leather and aftershave had made her nose tingle pleasantly. The feel of his warm breath on her face had sent a flash fire through her, and the subtle dominance of his big body made her crave contact with him.

Her "I'll come downstairs later," was her resistance to the temptation of all that. She couldn't let him get that close again. Though he was the only man she'd ever truly been attracted to—and had been foolish enough to love once—she had to avoid him.

All it took to shore up her resolve was the memory of how he'd looked at her just a few short days ago, his face hard as granite and his eyes cold with loathing. Her terror that he might find a reason to return to that harsh, unforgiving attitude was crippling. The mysterious flaw she carried, the one that made her unworthy of love and unlovable, made it impossible for her to believe the change in him was permanent. He'd regret this soon enough, then everything would be as it was before. If she trusted him now, it would destroy her.

Caitlin couldn't relax until she heard his boot steps move away from the door and go down the hall.

She checked the clock on her night table. It was only a few minutes until Mary served supper. She rose from the edge of the mattress and moved the pillows aside to remake the bed. She got her cane and walked carefully toward the door. Reno must have brought it to her room.

Though her foot hadn't been severely broken, it ached from the walking she'd already done that day. By the time she got downstairs, it was hurting and she favored it until she reached the dining room.

The moment Reno looked her way, she gritted her teeth and tried to conceal her discomfort. Her head was throbbing, but she made herself ignore it. Reno started to rise as if he meant to come around the table to help her with her chair, but she gave him a look that signaled her opposition to that idea.

He sat back down, but his gaze was sharp on her. It was as if he knew she was hiding her discomfort and was calculating how long she could keep it up. She eased onto the chair, relieved to sit down. The long trip from her room had tired her, and she was frustrated.

"If you put too much strain on that foot before it's ready, it might not heal right."

Caitlin didn't respond to that. Instead, she sat stiffly while Mary carried the food into the dining room.

The small burst of appetite surprised her, and Caitlin filled her plate, then cut into her steak. For the first time in what felt like weeks, food tasted good, and she ate as if she were starved.

Reno finished first and sat back with his coffee, staring. Caitlin tried to ignore his scrutiny.

"I want to hire a nurse." Reno's statement got her attention.

"I don't need one."

"You need someone to look after you."

Caitlin shook her head and looked down to spear the last bite of steak with her fork. "If I thought I needed a baby-sitter, I would have stayed in the hospital." She ate the bite, then set her fork down, painfully self-conscious now that Reno was focused so intensely on her.

"I sent your rental car back to San Antonio."

Caitlin's gaze shot to his. He'd guessed that she meant to leave the ranch, she could see it in his eyes. She dropped her hand to her lap and gripped the napkin.

"So you're taking over my life." Her voice was soft, but carried an edge of bitterness.

"You need someone to take care of you."

It was plain to Caitlin that the someone Reno had in mind was himself. A flash of anger made her pull her napkin from her lap and toss it to the table.

"I've been taking care of myself since I was eight

years old," she said, struggling to keep the pain of that out of her voice.

"Your mother died when you were eight?"

Reno had come back so fast with the question that she felt her breath catch. He was watching her more closely than ever and her eyes fled his.

"I don't feel like making conversation," she said coolly, then reached for her cane. She was halfway to her feet when Reno got up and came around the table to her.

He pulled the cane from her fingers and swept her up in his arms so fast that her head swam. She gasped and reflexively grabbed for his wide shoulders.

"You've been on that foot enough for one day."

Anger made her head pound. She struggled in his arms but he was walking to the hall door carrying her as if she weighed nothing.

"Put me down," she demanded, and emphasized the order by struggling harder.

Reno barely noticed her resistance. He carried her into the den, paused to kick the door closed, then carried her to the sofa. He sat down with her draped across his lap. Since he no longer had to carry her, he slipped his hand from under her knees and caught her hand. With her hand in his, he braced his forearm across her thighs to hold her still. He'd trapped her left elbow behind his shoulder, but not so tightly that he hurt her healing skin.

Caitlin was flooded with sensation. Reno's light restraint sent an avalanche of emotion through her, and the craving to be held more closely still made her shake as she fought it.

Frightened and furious, she burst out, "It always has to be your way, doesn't it?"

The angry words set off a flood of feelings that she suddenly couldn't stop and they came out in a torrent.

"Reno Duvall pities a kid, tosses her a few crumbs, then gets tired of her. He ignores her and makes her take it." Her eyes were blazing into the watchful depths of his. "His brother dies, she has the bad manners to live, and he decides she has to get out of his sight. One day, he orders her back, and when she gets there, he won't listen to anything she has to say. He won't let her talk, and once again the *universe* bends to his will. Then suddenly, he changes his mind, so she has to accept that, too. Right away he wants to run her life, and she'll bend to his will, by God, or he'll manhandle her until she does—"

The shameful sting of tears cut her off and she glared impotently at him through a blur so thick she couldn't see his face clearly.

His growling voice instantly took up where hers left off.

"Then, Reno Duvall decides he wants her—"

He leaned forward and his lips captured hers, enforcing his will and establishing his sexual dominance. He released her hand and moved his arm from her thighs to seize the back of her neck to prevent her retreat.

His mouth gentled suddenly on the soft lips he'd just parted. His tongue swept inside and worked with a seductive skill that banished her stiff resistance and robbed her of strength.

Caitlin felt herself slip rapidly into a tide of sensation and desire so hot and so intense that she felt faint. She was helpless to keep from responding to him. Her hand came up to his hard jaw, then slid back into his thick dark hair. A wildness shot through her and she clutched at him, hanging on for dear life as she pressed closer for everything she could get.

She'd never dreamed it could be like this. The shock of Reno's mouth on hers was matched only by the shock of his fingers releasing the buttons of her shirt. And then they were past the barrier of fabric, sliding expertly against her breast. She felt a ripple go through him at the discovery that the shoulder burn made her unable to tolerate wearing a bra. His tongue became more insistent as his fingers found the sensitive tip of her breast and toyed mercilessly with it.

He had seduced her so swiftly and with such shattering ease that she suddenly panicked. She yanked her hand from his hair and tried to pull his fingers away from her breast, but found herself clutching the back of his hand in an instinctive effort to urge him on. The violent clash of terror and craving jolted her.

Reno could destroy her. The thought streaked through her mind, and the frantic tingle of fear that went with it stopped her plunge toward disaster. She tried to break off the kiss, but Reno pressed his advantage.

The small jerking sob of fear and frustration that tore at her throat made him abruptly go still. She felt a tiny chill on her cheek and realized with fresh shock that her cheek was damp.

Shame made her drag her mouth from his and turn her face away to hide it. She was strangling on the tears she held back and she gasped for air so hard that her chest ached. She was so weak suddenly that she could barely sit upright. If not for the fact that Reno held her she would have collapsed. Her sensitized breast literally ached when his fingers eased away and he pulled his hand from beneath her blouse.

Her breath hitched and she gritted her teeth weakly to control it.

Reno's hand came up to her damp cheek and he gently pulled her against him. His arms came around her. He held her close and rested his jaw against her head. He didn't speak, but she sensed his anger.

Miraculously, it wasn't directed toward her but toward himself. She didn't know how she knew that, and she instantly doubted the impression.

Her whispered "Please, I want to go...to my room," broke in the middle of the words.

She understood none of this, and she was so confused that her head pounded with it. Her whole body pulsed with pain, and she knew she'd never be able to walk to her room under her own power.

And yet despite the ache, her body still trembled with the effects of Reno's kiss. Her blood still surged hotly with every beat of her heart. Exhaustion made her eyelids impossibly heavy and she could no longer keep them open.

When Reno carefully slipped his arm beneath her knees and lifted her, she stirred, but she settled against him as he stood. She drifted to sleep in the warm security of his arms, then stirred again when he sat her on the edge of her bed.

He released her, but instead of stepping back, she

felt his fingers working the rest of her buttons open. She grabbed his hands to stop him.

His gruff "I won't look," was terse.

Caitlin couldn't fight him, and sat mutely as he swiftly undressed her. She couldn't look at his face, but she knew he kept his word. She sensed he was looking away because she was so aware of him now that she would have been able to feel his gaze on her.

The moment he pulled her jeans off and only her underwear remained, he laid her down and dragged the covers over her. He stepped to the foot of the bed and pulled the sheet and spread aside to put the pillows near her feet. He lifted her cast to the pillows, then flipped the covers over it.

When he stepped back to her side, she looked up at him through heavy eyelids. His face was somber, but his eyes glowed with what she clearly recognized as possessiveness.

Because he could see she was looking at him, he spoke. "We'll go slower next time."

Caitlin squeezed her eyes closed and shook her head wearily. "There can't be a next time."

"There was always a next time for us, Caitlin," he said quietly. "You knew it as much as I did."

It shocked her to hear him say it, because in some strange way, she knew what he said was true. Whatever their history together, there'd always been a mysterious connection between them, something that bound them together and might always tie them in some way. Whatever the future held, whatever happened between them, there would always be some slim tendril of feeling between them. The knowledge

made her unbearably sad because she believed Reno
would always mean more to her than she could ever
mean to him.

She made a restless move of her head and turned
her face away. "I'm an easy conquest for you," she
said quietly. "That's what we've both always
known." The admission made her squeeze her eyes
closed.

Exhaustion made it impossible for her to mince
words. "For you, this is just lust. Once it burns out,
whatever we've done will be just one more thing I'll
have to live with." She took a steadying breath because she wasn't strong enough to hold back the tide
of pain. "And I'm tired of living with things after
they go wrong."

The silence that followed was heavy. She felt the
prickle of tears and tried to summon a last bit of
strength to keep them back.

She hadn't heard Reno move, but she felt the warm
gust of his breath on her cheek when he leaned down.
Startled, she turned her head and gasped when her
lips brushed his.

"Sleep now, baby, get well." His lips were so
tender on hers, so persuasive that she lay there, helpless against the warm flood that spread through her,
too weak against him to turn her face away. She
couldn't fight the love that welled up from something
deep in her heart, she could only feel it take her over
as she tried to withstand the terrible sadness of discovering it was there.

"You'll learn to trust me, and everything will come

right.'' The rough words were a vow that Caitlin didn't dare let herself believe.

Her soft ''no'' was silenced softly by a last gentle kiss.

Reno left the room then and closed the door. She was so exhausted, so overwhelmed by the torment of her feelings, that she fell instantly into the refuge of sleep.

Caitlin was right. It did always have to be his way. Reno hadn't thought much about it before. He'd been in charge since he was seventeen, shouldering the work and the responsibility, making the hard decisions, taking the risks, until the tendency to lead and dominate became such a natural part of the man he was and the way he lived that he never questioned it.

Until he'd forced his will on Caitlin.

Her resistance that day had frustrated him, but the way she'd pushed herself while she was so weak and in pain had frustrated him more.

He'd been compelled to take over, compelled to take *her* over with that kiss. He'd meant to go slow with her. His hatred had hurt her, but if she could ever get over it, he could accept that it might take a long time.

But the moment he had her in his arms, then on his lap, all his good intentions had vanished. The tension that had been building between them since the day she'd come back to Coulter City exploded. For Caitlin, years of hurt and hunger had been the catalyst, for him it had been lust.

And yet he knew it was more than just lust. As

he'd declared to her, there was a connection between them, a bond of some kind. A tie that went beyond the events of the past, yet managed to exist in spite of it all.

He'd been wrong to force the kiss when she was too weak and too confused to handle it. The guilt of what he'd done was almost as strong as the fierce satisfaction he'd got from her helpless response to him. Because she *had* responded to him, deeply and completely until her insecurities had frightened her off.

Some things, some people, were now forever beyond his reach. His feelings for Caitlin—and Caitlin herself—were alive and vital and still with him.

He'd almost lost her, too. Once because he couldn't give her a chance, and once in the fire. He wouldn't risk losing her again. He refused to lose her because she was afraid to trust him.

Before he went to bed, Reno went into her room, set the intercom so he could hear if she woke up in the night, then stood looking down at her. She was sleeping deeply and peacefully. She'd get well, she'd recover her strength, but her heart would take the longest to heal. Those wounds were the worst because they'd festered a long time and likely ran clear to her soul.

Common sense warned him she might never heal, but hope made him think about the steady medicine of patience, time...and love.

CHAPTER EIGHT

CAITLIN slept late that next morning. She removed the cast briefly to shower and wash her hair. By the time she got dressed and started downstairs, she was already tiring.

The frustration of it made her restless. She got to the kitchen just before 9:00 a.m. and Mary greeted her pleasantly. Caitlin was grateful to be able to eat breakfast alone. After that kiss, she dreaded seeing Reno again, though she was resigned to it. After discovering how easily she tired, common sense warned that she shouldn't rush away from the Broken B until she was stronger. It was difficult to accept, but she was forced to make peace with the idea.

Morning in the big house was quiet. Air-conditioning made the bright sunshine that streamed in the windows feel comfortable. The sound of Mary rattling silverware and dishes made her think of the days before Jess had hired indoor help, the days when her mother cooked all the meals, did all the baking, kept the house immaculate, yet made time for her small daughter.

After all the heartache she'd known here, there was something about being alone in the big house that comforted her, something that reminded her so strongly of her mother and those early times when she'd felt loved, that the thought of leaving forever suddenly made her feel sad. She hadn't felt this way a few days ago when the house had seemed large and empty and lonely.

Something had changed in her, something small but significant. How much it had to do with Reno changing his mind about her—and what had happened between them last night—was a question she was afraid to answer.

Instead, she wondered how many of these sentimental feelings were due to these sudden memories of her mother. Though she couldn't clearly picture her face, she remembered the strong sense of her mother's love, the warm feeling of security.

Unfortunately, the only real security she'd felt since her mother had been in Reno's arms last night. The realization sent a fresh tingle of anxiety through her. She'd made up her mind not to need anyone, to live out the rest of her life keeping everyone at a distance.

But Reno had kissed her and made mincemeat of her resolve. She'd thought she was too frigid for a single kiss to have that kind of effect on her, but he'd proved her wrong. Why was it that the only man who'd actually managed to arouse her was the man who was the most potentially lethal to her?

Or was the reason for her frigid sexuality the fact that she'd always known that Reno was the only man for her? It was a fact that any man she'd ever dated stood in the shade of Reno's strong personality and physical appeal. If that was true, she was in deep trouble.

You'll learn to trust me, he'd said. Though her will

declared she never would, her heart had trembled with the longing to do just that. The torment of the two reactions kept her unsettled and vulnerable.

By the time she finished breakfast and got up to sit in the shade on the patio, she was tired again. Frustration made her grab her cane and hat and walk through the house to the front door instead. Cast or not, she'd walk a ways up the long driveway. She needed to rebuild her strength and do something about this troubling lack of stamina. If she pushed herself, she'd get stronger.

When she got stronger, she could leave. As she stepped out into the hot sunshine and tugged her hat down to shade her face, she felt the poignant ache of leaving her mother's house forever.

Oh, God, what was wrong with her? Why was everything suddenly so intensely emotional and painfully sentimental? As she stepped carefully off the big verandah onto the walk, she realized that her injuries might be the cause. She wasn't feeling well, and the pressure and upheaval of everything that had happened was bound to upset her.

She tried to ignore the reminder that she'd struggled with her emotions since she'd come back to Texas and that she hadn't been doing very well with them even before she'd been injured in the fire.

Reno was riding in from the big pasture west of the headquarters when he caught sight of someone walking up the ranch drive in the direction of the highway. He recognized Caitlin immediately and felt a rush of anger. Even at a distance, he could tell she was exhausted. Her steps seemed to shorten with each one she took. Likely, she'd pushed herself too far and was just starting to realize it. The moment he saw her stop and turn carefully to walk back, he rode his horse to the nearest gate.

Once he was through and the gate was secure, he galloped the sorrel through the ranch yard and onto the grassy shoulder of the graveled drive. She'd stopped walking by the time he reached her and his horse slid to a halt.

"What in hell do you think you're doing?"

He saw the faint spasm of hurt in her eyes and instantly regretted his harshness. He urged the sorrel close and leaned down to hold his hand out to her. "Come on up," he said, his voice gruff. "You can ride easier than you can walk."

Caitlin's tired gaze dropped from his to the big hand he held out to her. She'd walked too far and now the stretch of driveway between where she stood and the house seemed miles long. She was nauseous and her head was pounding. She couldn't seem to make a right choice about anything, and this new choice seemed rife with emotional consequences.

"Give me your hand, Caitlin."

The quiet order was more a request than a demand, and that surprised her. Her weary gaze must have signaled her surprise because the hard line of his mouth gentled into a faint curve.

He gave the reins one quick wrap around the saddle horn, then leaned toward her. Instead of taking her hand, he caught her waist and lifted her to sit across his lap. Finding herself back in the same position as the night before made her feel wary and self-conscious.

"Relax," he growled. "Too many people around for me to try much." He turned his horse, and walked him slowly back to the house, but instead of setting her down at the end of the walk, he rode the sorrel across the grass to the verandah steps.

He set her on the wood floor, then straightened. His eyes moved over her grimly. For an instant, she thought he'd say something about her walk. She sensed his disapproval and frustration, but in the end, he said nothing. He reached up and touched his hat brim in a silent gesture of respect, then turned the sorrel and rode off.

Caitlin watched him go, her emotions in an uproar over the short ride and the thrill of being in Reno's arms.

When Reno went to the house for lunch, he found Caitlin in the living room, asleep in the recliner. He didn't wake her. He ate in the kitchen then checked her again before he left the house. Mary would keep lunch until she was ready to eat, and she'd promised to keep an eye on Caitlin. He'd feel better with a trained nurse in the house, but Caitlin had made her thoughts on the subject clear.

When he came to the house for supper, she was awake. They sat across from each other in the dining room, and it reassured him to see her eat. He was careful not to say anything that might disturb her and affect her appetite. She'd never eaten much during the few meals he'd shared with her before, so he considered the fact that she was now eating normally to be a good sign.

She was still wary of him and on guard. He couldn't have missed the fine edge of tension about her. So he talked to her about the ranch and what was going on with it. She kept silent, but he could tell she was interested. He truly was going to give her the ranch and everything else, but he sensed that reminding her of it now might upset her.

He'd told her before the fire that he was going to give it all to her, but he'd made the gesture sound like something he'd hoped would cause her misery. No reason to remind her of that either.

After supper, Caitlin left the table. She went into the living room and switched on the TV. He glanced in later to see that she was watching a news program, but he didn't intrude. Later, he heard her go upstairs to bed and he gave up all pretense of doing book work.

He was trying not to crowd her, but he was already tired of it. Caitlin was a self-sufficient woman who'd lived most of her life apart from others. If he let her, she might continue on the same way the rest of her life.

And he wanted her too much to let that happen. The strong streak of impatience in him made it impossible to tolerate much more of Caitlin's remoteness.

As it turned out, Reno was forced to be patient. The first week, Caitlin slept a lot and as far as he knew, didn't try any more walks up the driveway. Nearly every time he came to the house, she was resting. Sometimes she chose the recliner in the living room, sometimes she was upstairs in her room or on the lounge chair on the verandah out front. The only time he saw her was at supper. She was quiet during the meal, making only minimal responses to any attempt he made at conversation. She was on guard against him, but she wasn't up to a repeat of her first night home from the hospital, so he'd allowed her to keep her distance.

He watched her those next days, relieved when the faint circles beneath her eyes became a bit less dark. He could tell when her headaches began to get better, because when she came to the table one evening, she seemed less tense and her eyes were a little brighter. Two days after that, he noticed that she didn't lean quite so much of her weight on her cane.

Lucky, Bob and Tar came by one evening a week after she'd gotten out of the hospital. He'd gone to the den, leaving the four of them in the living room. Dean Carnes and his wife wanted to see her to thank her in person for carrying their boy out of the fire, but Reno had held them off. Finally, the night after Lucky and the others visited, he brought up the subject at supper.

"You seem to be getting stronger," he remarked casually.

Caitlin's gaze came up to touch his before it returned to her plate. He saw the faint glimmer in her eyes that hinted at secrecy and sensed she was planning to leave the ranch as soon as she was well enough. He'd make sure all of the ranch vehicles were unavailable to her, and if he had to, he'd hire every rental car in a two-hundred-mile radius to keep her from getting one. He'd have a talk with Mary and Lucky so she'd be thwarted if she turned to them.

"Dean Carnes and his wife have been waiting to come to the house until you feel up to a visit."

Caitlin hesitated, her fork partway to her mouth. She lowered the fork to rest the side of her hand next to her plate. "I'd rather they didn't."

She sensed Reno's disapproval. "You saved their kid's life. They feel bad about how they acted before."

Caitlin shook her head. "Anyone could have found the boy. If I hadn't gone in, one of the men would have." She lifted the fork and took the bite of food.

"Anyone might have," he agreed, "but you were the one who did. The Carnes are crazy about their kids, and it's no small thing to them that you saved Billy's life." He paused when she shook her head, more adamantly this time. "Part of the obligation of heroes and heroines is to allow people to express their gratitude."

"I'm no heroine." She set her fork aside and plucked her napkin off her lap to lift it to the table.

"You probably don't want to be, but that doesn't change the facts." He watched as she slid her chair back to stand and reached for her cane. He set down his own fork, frustrated with her.

"I've seen you lots of ways, Caitlin, but you've never been rude or ungracious. Or cruel."

Reno's stern words made her glance at him. The

solemn look in his eyes snared her. "This is important to the Carnes."

Caitlin glanced away, feeling trapped. She didn't want to face the Carnes family, didn't really want to have to face anyone. Over these last days, she'd drawn into herself more and more until she was eager to be on her way, to go someplace where no one knew her, and live anonymously while she tried to make some kind of life for herself. Having to see the Carnes, having to bear their gratitude and perhaps their apologies, was excruciating. To someone as naturally reserved as she was, the idea of attracting such attention was horrifying.

Reno's voice was low. "Give them a chance, Caitlin." His persuasive tone made her unbearably restless.

"When do they want to come and how long do you think they'll be here?"

Reno's lips curved slightly. "They'll be here in about ten minutes, and they'll probably not stay long. Dean's not much for words. I don't know about his wife, but neither of them will want to tire you."

Caitlin nodded, electing to let go by the information that the Carnes would be there in ten minutes. Obviously, Reno had already set up the meeting without consulting her, but now that everyone expected her to do this, it was probably better to get it over with right away. She felt herself give in.

Her strained "I'll be in the living room," underscored how difficult she thought it would be.

Reno watched as she turned and walked from the room.

*   *   *

The Carnes' visit was mercifully brief, but managed to leave Caitlin emotional. The moment Mrs. Carnes and her husband came into the room, she walked over to where Caitlin stood with her cane and caught her in a brief hug. Caitlin awkwardly returned it. She felt huge relief when the woman released her and stepped back, though she took hold of Caitlin's free hand with hers.

"We're sorry about how we acted when you caught our boys in the loft, Miz Bodine," Mrs. Carnes said, gripping Caitlin's fingers urgently. "If we'd done the right thing then, been grateful to you and punished the boys properly, they might never have started the fire." Her face crumpled. "And there's no way to tell you how grateful we are that you saved Billy." Tears streamed down the woman's face.

Both of them watched her expectantly. Uncomfortable, Caitlin tried to say something to minimize what she'd done. "I—I was glad I could get to him."

She waited a moment for Mrs. Carnes to regain control of her tears. The woman released her hand to reach into a skirt pocket for a tissue. "I'm sorry to bawl all over you, ma'am, but I'll never get over being grateful to have both my sons alive. And it's gonna take us a long time to get over the guilt, both for how we acted toward you, and the guilt of the barn burning down."

The cowboy interrupted grimly. "If you'd rather I quit the ranch and moved on, we'd understand and hold no hard feelin's."

The offer shocked Caitlin. "There's no need for you to quit." She glanced helplessly at Reno, who stood by watching. "Mr. Duvall considers you a valuable employee. I don't understand how there could be a problem with you staying on." Because the cowboy seemed unconvinced, Caitlin added softly, "Please, Mr. Carnes, stay on. A good man isn't easy to replace."

Dean Carnes looked down at his hat, gripping it uneasily as fiery color spread up his lean cheeks to his hairline. Finally, he nodded, then glanced up at her before his gaze flicked quickly to Reno's. "If you're sure about this, then I thank you, Miz Bodine. Good jobs aren't easy to replace either. It'll be an honor to work for you."

Before Caitlin could correct him, Mrs. Carnes stepped forward to thank her again for saving little Billy. Uncomfortable with their gratitude, Caitlin made herself smile and endure it until the Carnes left the house.

The moment they were gone, Caitlin started for the hall to escape to the verandah. The Carnes' visit had unsettled her and she was relieved it was over. She also wanted to get away from Reno.

Just as she reached the hall door, he called after her. "You've got a doctor's appointment in the morning at ten. I'll come back to the house and drive you."

She nodded and stepped into the hall. She'd be glad to see the doctor. Though she was feeling better, she still tired easily. When she stepped out the front door, she walked to the wide wooden swing on the verandah and sat down wearily.

The headaches weren't as bad as they had been, but they hung on. Her recovery was slow, and it frustrated her as much as it worried her. Perhaps the strain of being in the house, of avoiding Reno, was draining her. If he was the cause of her fatigue, she could follow through with her plans to leave the Broken B and be confident that she'd feel better right away. But if she was still battling the lingering effects of the concussion, she'd be sensible to stay on a bit longer.

And if she had to stay, she wasn't certain how long she could keep avoiding Reno. He'd left her to herself these past few days, but she'd sensed his impatience. She'd seen the intense looks he'd given her, and there'd been no way to ignore the smoldering gleam in his eyes when she'd caught his gaze wandering over her. She'd been grateful that he hadn't touched her again, but if she stayed, how long would that last?

She'd given up pushing herself to get well that first full day out of the hospital when she'd walked up the drive and Reno had brought her back. It really had been too soon then, but maybe it wasn't now. She had to do something besides rest to get back her strength. Thinking about the way Reno looked at her sometimes and the wild flutter of excitement she felt whenever he did, made her realize she needed to hurry.

She was starting to think too much about where all those intense looks and flutters of excitement might lead. She knew in her head they could only lead to disaster. Unfortunately, her heart wasn't as strongly convinced.

At the doctor's office the next day, she asked to be allowed to start horseback riding, but the doctor cautioned her about too much jostling and the danger of another blow to the head so soon after the concussion. Because he could tell she was determined to ride, he finally agreed to a very limited time each day on horseback at a smooth-gaited walk.

The black gelding was a perfect choice for that, and Caitlin felt her spirits lift. The doctor had no quick solution for her fatigue, but he'd told her to expect it for at least a few more weeks, though it would get steadily better now.

Reno was livid when she told him about her plans to start riding. His growling "You will *not* ride," came out through gritted teeth and was followed by an eloquent string of curses, along with a very explicit outline of what he wanted to do to the doctor.

His vitriol shocked her, but the protectiveness behind his invective gave her a warm sense of safety and security. His fierceness was in keeping with his strong personality and his natural compulsion to protect the ones he cared for. She couldn't help that she responded instantly to it, or that her effort to dismiss his upset on her behalf fell flat.

She craved so many things that Reno seemed capable of giving her, and not even the reminder that it was foolish to crave them from him was enough to stop the wanting. The only sure way to stop it was to leave the ranch.

Reno announced at breakfast that next morning that she could spend the morning with him.

"If you're so determined to push yourself, you might as well have something productive to do."

She saw right off that there was no way for her to

turn him down that wouldn't make him suspicious. She'd overheard a conversation he'd had with Mary the afternoon before which had ended with "I want to know the second she makes any calls." He'd carried a cell phone ever since, so it was clear that the very least he expected was that she'd try to call a car rental agency. Perhaps if she spent the morning with Reno he'd let down his guard.

Caitlin went along with him to the cookhouse, then kept to herself near the door while he went over the day's work assignments with the men. Several of the men didn't realize she was present until they turned to go out.

Reno got a pickup and they drove out to make the rounds of stock tanks and windmills. He wouldn't allow her to get out to open and close the gates, but because the pickup had an automatic transmission, he let her drive it through while he worked the gates.

Reno drove slowly to avoid a bumpy ride, and they left the windows down while it was still relatively cool. Caitlin welcomed the warm, fresh morning air and found herself slowly relaxing with him. While they checked stock tanks, they looked over the cattle. Reno used the cell phone to report a couple of cows that needed a closer look, but they kept on the move all morning. Caitlin ignored the mild headache that persisted. It felt so good to be out of the house that she was afraid to mention it to Reno.

By the time they drove back to the ranch house at noon, Caitlin was fighting to stay awake. The long morning had exhausted her, though all she'd done was ride in the truck and occasionally drive it through an open gate.

Reno parked in the drive near the back patio, but when she got out and was about to step off the running board, he caught her and swung her into his arms. He looked down into her flushed face. A half smile curved his handsome mouth.

"Flash those blue eyes at me, honey, call me bad names, but I'm going to manhandle you all the way to the kitchen."

The outrageous words startled a laugh out of her that made his smile widen gently.

"And as long as everything has to be my way, I'd like to see more smiles. Improves the scenery."

The lightness between them sparked a sudden feeling of closeness that Caitlin found irresistible. She'd never seen Reno like this, and she was fascinated by this hint of a new side to his stern personality. He'd caught her so by surprise that she could only stare.

His expression sobered a little and his voice went low. "If you keep looking at me like that, I won't care if someone sees what I do next."

Caitlin felt heat flood her cheeks and she looked away from him. Reno intended to begin again what he'd started with that kiss her first night home from the hospital. She got the message loud and clear, and the sweet warmth that pulsed through her made her tremble with as much anticipation as fear.

Reno's arms tightened on her briefly before he started toward the house. Caitlin held on, stealing a glance at his rugged face as she felt herself being drawn deeper into the vortex of his strong appeal.

She took a long nap that afternoon and awoke feeling relaxed and a little stronger. Reno came to the house at four o'clock and found her sitting on the verandah by the front door. He stepped outside.

"I gave Mary the night off. I thought we might go into Coulter City for supper."

Caitlin tensed and he saw it. "No need to dress up. If you feel like it, we might catch a movie after."

She looked away from him and focused into the distance. "That isn't a good idea." And it wasn't. The terrible rush of joy and excitement that had burst up at his suggestion was something she felt compelled to resist.

Reno walked over to her and crouched down by her chair. "You can't say no," he pointed out quietly. That got her attention and made her look at him.

"It's just supper, maybe a movie. Someplace away from here, someplace public. Would do us both good to get out."

Caitlin's gaze fell from his. The someplace public part was something she'd rather avoid. She didn't want to attract anyone's notice. Just because Reno seemed to have changed his mind about her didn't mean anyone else had. The opposite kind of notice— like that of the salon owner the day she'd gotten out of the hospital—was almost as bad. She hated to be thought of as a heroine almost as much as she hated for people to think she was a murderess.

Reno's low voice was somber. "You've got to face people sometime, Caitlin. You've lived your life in the shadows too long."

His perception rattled her and she looked at him. "I'd rather live in the shadows."

Reno glanced away from her a moment, as if he were framing his next words. When he looked back at her, the intensity in his eyes made her gaze waver.

"It's safer, maybe. But lonesome."

Caitlin's gaze did slip from his then. Reno's words pushed at her and she had to deflect them. "Loneliness doesn't bother me."

"It bothers you every minute," he said quietly.

The accurate statement made her restless. She started to reach for her cane, but Reno caught her hand.

"Loneliness bothers me, too. I get tired of it."

Reno's admission made her look at him. The intensity was back in his eyes and he lifted his hand to run the back of a finger down her cheek. "It's only dinner."

Caitlin couldn't help the confusion of her feelings. She'd tried so hard to stay away from Reno, tried so hard to resist his appeal. But after spending a good part of the day with him, the craving to be close to him was powerful. And he was touching her, sending her thoughts into chaos and her emotions into a mad whirl. It was suddenly impossible to tell him no.

CHAPTER NINE

THE restaurant Reno took her to was one of the finest in Coulter City. She'd worn a blue silk blouse with long sleeves and white cotton slacks. Reno had worn a dark suit jacket over his Western shirt and stone-washed jeans. Together, they looked casual, but well-dressed enough to fit in with some of the diners who were more elegantly dressed. They were led to an out-of-the-way table right away because Reno had made reservations.

Caitlin felt self-conscious with her cane as they crossed the room. Several of the seated diners looked up as they passed, and the hurried whispers in their wake increased her discomfort. When they reached their table, Reno pulled her chair out and seated her before he took the chair beside her. Their backs were to the wall, so they had a clear view of most of the restaurant. Caitlin caught sight of her cousin's blond head several tables away and felt her discomfort increase.

Madison was staring at her, her blue gaze searching Caitlin's face for a few moments before she abruptly looked away. Caitlin looked away, too, jolted by her cousin's presence.

Madison St. John hated upset of any kind, and her cousin, Caitlin Bodine, seemed to be a steady source.

Knowing Caitlin had returned for her father's funeral—and seeing her there—had brought back strong memories of Beau Duvall.

Those memories were poignant and upsetting enough, but the memories Caitlin had stirred about their childhood together were even more poignant and upsetting. Madison didn't want to remember how much she and Caitlin had meant to each other once, how much they'd relied on each other for the love and support and sense of family their caretakers had been incapable of giving them.

Madison had been terrified when she returned from New York three weeks ago and found out about the fire and Caitlin's injuries. She'd agonized over whether to send flowers or whether she could forgive Caitlin enough to visit. The dilemma had torn her apart. But when the crisis passed and she found out that Caitlin would be all right, she'd ended up doing nothing.

They'd been as close as sisters once, inseparable until Beau had come between them. Madison never let herself think about how much she missed her cousin, because the truth was, she'd missed her terribly. When she thought about Caitlin, she inevitably thought about the reason for their break, and when she let herself think about that, she was reminded of Beau.

Even now, as she sat alone at her reserved table, it was hard not to be reminded of Beau and the terrible way he'd died. She'd heard that Reno no longer held Caitlin responsible for Beau's death—and because they were together in the restaurant tonight, it must be true—but Madison wasn't able to be so forgiving. Because of Caitlin, everything she'd wanted had been taken away from her, everything bright and beautiful, until all she had left was money and things and frivolous little obsessions.

She'd managed to fill her life with expensive possessions to make up for what she'd lost, but it was at times like these, when she was forced to think about Caitlin and Beau, that all of the rich, wonderful things her grandmother's money could buy suddenly seemed like so much tinsel and frosting.

Knowing she couldn't think about how shallow and secretly desperate her life had become, she caught the waiter's eye and gave him an impatient signal. When he arrived, she distracted herself from her pain at his expense, launching into a minor tirade about the salad, the wine and the abysmal lack of service, *his* in particular.

It made her feel important when he rushed off with her salad and wine in his haste to replace them with something more suitable. When he returned and set them before her so solicitously, he made her feel cared for, cosseted.

He never guessed that she felt excruciating guilt for her pitiful little game. But he'd waited on her many times before, so he knew how the script went. He played his part well, lavishing her with attention and creating the illusion of devotion as he hovered nearby to mollify her complaints and cater to her every whim.

But then, he knew she always left him a huge tip, rarely less than a fifty-dollar bill. He was like everyone else in Coulter City who lusted after her money. They all allowed her to play her rich bitch role to the hilt because they wanted her money.

No one wanted *her*, no one but Caitlin and Beau had ever wanted her. But Beau was dead and she wasn't sure her memories of him made it possible for her to mend things with Caitlin. No one but the two of them had ever seemed to notice she was alive or cared a thing for her until her grandmother passed away and left her a mansion and a fortune.

Madison's revenge for being valued only for her money was to put everyone who wanted it through the ordeal of tolerating her to get it. The more money they hoped to get, the more she put them through.

The real truth was that if anyone ever truly cared about what happened to her, or found something about her they could genuinely love, they could have every dollar and diamond she owned.

Madison felt the shame of lonely tears gathering behind her eyes. She glanced speculatively toward the waiter and considered the crisp fifty-dollar bill in her handbag.

Caitlin eventually relaxed and managed to ignore her cousin's presence, but she felt untold relief when Madison finished her meal and swept out of the restaurant.

Reno was the perfect host. He drew her into a discussion about what she'd been doing these past years, and he'd seemed impressed with what little she felt comfortable telling him about the SC Ranch in Montana.

They'd finished their meal when Reno brought up the Broken B.

"I'm transferring the Broken B and all of Jess's holdings to you."

Caitlin glanced over at him in surprise.

"I've got a lawyer looking into tax liabilities to see what the cheapest way is," he went on. "If the liability goes too high, I'll look into making you a partner, and then gradually switch ownership of everything over to you. But you'll be in charge and benefit from the profits right away."

Caitlin picked up her napkin and rubbed it roughly over her lips, panicked. She set the napkin aside and shook her head. "I can't accept it."

Reno seemed unperturbed by her refusal. He leaned back in his chair and casually raised his left arm to rest it across the back of her chair. "You're the only heir Jess should have named. Everything he owned is yours by birth and by moral right."

Caitlin shook her head again and looked at him. "Everything Jess owned was his to do with as he pleased. He made his wishes clear in his will. Besides, the results of the blood test haven't come back."

"Some wishes shouldn't be honored," he said grimly. "And that damned blood test was meant to hurt you, so I don't really give a damn what it shows. Whether you were Jess's natural daughter or not, you were raised with his name, so whatever he owned belongs to you."

Caitlin was stunned. "I can't accept it."

"And I don't want it," he argued gruffly. "Any of

it. I've got my own place, I don't need to take what rightfully belongs to you.''

She continued to shake her head. ''Your generosity is commendable, but everything belongs to you. I can't accept it.''

Reno leaned toward her and eased his arm off the chair back onto her shoulders. ''You're not going to fight me on this, Caitlin.''

She looked at him again, defiance shining through her shock. ''You can't give me something I won't take.''

Reno leaned even closer. ''I'll give you anything I damned well please,'' he growled, and managed to make it sound like a sensual threat.

Flustered, Caitlin glanced away from him and reached for her water glass for a sip. Her head was whirling.

''Would you like dessert now? Or later?''

The quick switch of subject jolted her. Her ''Whatever you'd like,'' came out sounding breathless as she set her glass down.

Reno's low chuckle sent an avalanche of pleasurable tingles over her skin.

''I've got a feeling the *universe* is about to bend to my will,'' he said in a rough whisper.

His subtle revision of her words the other night made Caitlin turn her head. Her eyes flew to his.

But Reno had looked from her to signal the waiter. When he rushed to their table, Reno prompted her to choose a dessert.

Still shocked, Caitlin gave in, ordering a dessert while her mind frantically searched for a way to refuse Reno's generosity. But when she felt Reno's strong fingers gently stroking her shoulder and she glanced his way, she saw the smoldering intent in his gaze. She realized instantly that Reno had much more in mind than their dispute over Jess's will.

After they left the restaurant, Reno took her to a movie at the new multiplex on the edge of Coulter City. They agreed on a suspense film. Caitlin was hoping it would take both their minds off their mutual attraction, but the strong chemistry between the lead actor and actress—and the steamy love scene—only managed to make things worse.

She'd never been particularly affected by a movie love scene, but she was suddenly sensitive to it. It didn't help that Reno's arm rested possessively across the back of her seat or that he'd reached over with his other hand to catch her fingers and toy absently with them.

By the time they got out of the theater Caitlin's emotions were wildly excited. The fact that Reno settled his arm around her waist and kept her solidly against his tall, hard body all the way to the car sent a tortuous longing through her.

She was grateful when their seat belts ensured their physical separation. But the moment Reno turned onto the highway for home, he reached for her hand and gripped it gently. The electric sensations between them sent a new rush of excitement through her.

In spite of the distance she'd tried to maintain these last days, her feelings for Reno had deepened dangerously. Tonight they'd gone deeper still. Her heart was in a turmoil of fear and soaring hope. The craving to trust Reno was strong, but her deep belief that his interest in her was temporary made everything painful for her.

She dreaded what might happen when they got back to the ranch, and realized that whatever happened, it would be her fault. If she'd refused to go with Reno tonight and avoided him more persistently, there would be none of this edgy anticipation. There would also be no terrifying fear and no wild, sweet hope to heighten it.

She sensed Reno's expectation, saw it every time his eyes met hers. She felt it in the languorous way his fingers traced over the back on her hand. Caitlin felt herself melting, felt a longing so forceful and primal come over her that she was losing her ability to withstand it.

By the time Reno parked his car in the drive near the front of the house, it was all she could do to sit rigidly in her seat and not look at him.

Without a word, Reno switched off the lights and the engine, then got out of the car. Caitlin's eyes followed him in the security lights of the ranch headquarters as he walked around the front of the car to her door. Neither of them spoke as he opened the door and she stepped out. Reno took her cane and slid his arm around her waist for their silent walk to the front door.

When they stepped inside, the house was still and dark. Only dim light from outside penetrated the thick sheer panels that had been drawn closed for the night.

Reno led them partway into the entry hall before he stopped and turned toward her in the dimness.

He reached up and removed his Stetson, tossing it toward the hall table. Caitlin tried to step back, but he tightened his arm around her waist and drew her close.

"I want you, Caitlin." Reno's voice was rough and persuasive. He lowered his head and his lips stroked warmly over hers. "More than I ever wanted any woman, I want you."

Caitlin swayed dizzily, and her fingers gripped his arms. His lips teased gently over hers, and she turned her head slightly to break the contact. Reno pulled her closer and his lips persisted. His mouth captured hers tenderly, and his hand came up to the back of her head to hold her steady for the sensual onslaught.

Caitlin was lost that very moment and her hands slid up the sleeves of his suit jacket to his shoulders. Emotion flooded up, love and longing surged through her as she returned his kiss.

Suddenly Reno shifted and he swept her into his arms. His lips parted hers and his tongue pressed inside for a long unhurried taste before it retreated, sending a jolt of sensuality through her that made her weak. And then he was walking through the darkened house.

She was floating on an ocean of warm sensation. She was dimly aware that Reno had started up the staircase. Startled, she tore her mouth from his and pressed it against his hard shoulder. Reno continued effortlessly up the stairs and the steady rhythm of his

boots on the upstairs hall made her shiver with anticipation.

Sanity was a distant concept. What could it hurt
now if they became intimate? She'd already lost her
heart to Reno. There'd never really been a question.
She loved him now because she'd always loved him.
The sad truth was that she always would.

By the time Reno carried her into her room, the
inevitability of what would happen between them im-
pacted her, distracting her from her fears. By next
week, next month, or next year, she'd be alone, and
she and Reno would again be estranged. That lingering fear, that terrible certainty, went too deep for her
to ignore or discount.

But what would it really hurt to have this one time
with Reno, and maybe another, then another? As terrified as she was to let him that close, something broken and lost in her suddenly needed to survive,
needed to make that deep physical and emotional connection to another human being, to Reno. The need
was clamoring too loudly and too insistently for her
to silence it.

Reno strode across the floor to her bed. He braced
a knee on the mattress and laid her across the bedspread. His big body followed her down and his
mouth found hers again for a long, feverish kiss.

The hot pulse in her throat was choking her, stifling
the last of her fears, the last of her resistance. The
pulse spread through her blood, heating it and sending
it faster and faster through her veins.

Reno's fingers swiftly dispatched the buttons of her
blouse and slipped inside. He encountered the lace of

her bra and groaned with masculine frustration before he expertly unhooked it. And then his big hand covered her breast. His tongue pressed past her lips and Caitlin could only cling to him and return what his mouth did to hers.

She was drowning in sensation and love. It was at just the moment Caitlin thought she would faint that Reno dragged his hand from her breast and braced it beside her. His mouth increased its demand those next seconds, until he began to ease its pressure.

What followed were several drugging moments as his lips lavished hers with unhurried passion. Eventually, his mouth left hers and he slid down until his lips found her breast. Caitlin speared her fingers greedily into his thick hair and gasped raggedly at the new intimacy.

Too soon, Reno turned his head and rested his rough cheek against her hot skin. They were both shaking with the force of desire, but Reno established his dominance by reclaiming control of them both. He recovered far more quickly than she could, and lifted his head to loom over her in the darkness.

"You belong to me, Caitlin Bodine. You belong *with* me." He lowered his head to place a soft, lingering kiss on her lips. "And if I don't leave this bed right now, we're gonna find more proof." He stopped teasing her lips with his to add, "Unless you need more proof."

Caitlin knew what he was asking. The need to go the whole way, the compulsion to connect as deeply and completely with Reno as it was possible for a man and a woman to be connected was overwhelming in those next wild heartbeats of time.

But if they made love now, Caitlin truly would belong to Reno. Completely. If they made love now, she'd lose her last choice and would commit herself to him so deeply she would never be the same.

The awful truth was that she was still terrified to give herself to him. If he hadn't stopped just now… Suddenly, she wasn't ready to find out how quickly his lust would cool once he could have her, or how quickly what he felt for her would ebb.

He'd only used the word "want," had only said she "belonged" to him, belonged *with* him. He hadn't used the word love, hadn't made any emotional declarations or pledged any permanent vows. He'd only used possessive terms and, if she was smart, she'd not read anything too significant or lasting into them.

Her whispered "I don't need more proof," was devastatingly true. But she wasn't only talking about belonging to him, she was also talking about the painful lessons she'd learned long before this.

It hurt when he eventually stopped his long, slow kisses. It hurt even more when he eased himself off her, then off the bed.

Caitlin lay limply, feeling the chill that gusted over her without the heat of his body against hers. He left the room then, closing the door softly on his way out.

The next morning, Caitlin woke at sunrise, but stayed in her room until she was certain Reno had finished breakfast and left the house for the morning. He would naturally think that the day before had been tiring for her, and that their late night was something she needed to rest up from.

Every insecurity she'd ever had was making itself felt, every fear, every worry, every doubt had been stirred up. Her heart was heavy, and the sadness she felt was the worst of her life.

If it was this bad now, what would it have been like if she'd made love with Reno last night? The question pounded at her. And how much worse would it be if they'd made love, and she was sitting here now, believing that the countdown to Reno's fading interest had begun?

The treachery of her own heart made her feel ill. She'd been so close to giving herself to Reno last night, her heart had all but talked her into it. The moment she was in his arms and he was kissing her, she'd not been able to think straight. If Reno hadn't eased away and taken control...

The feeling that she had to leave the Broken B— to leave Texas—had never been as strong as it was that moment.

She showered and dressed for the day, then went downstairs for breakfast. Her appetite was gone again, and after Mary left the kitchen, she finally gave up and carried her plate and silverware to the sink to rinse them.

Reno came into the kitchen from the back door and walked directly to where she stood facing the counter. He pulled off his Stetson and tossed it next to the sink. His hands slid around her from behind and he pressed against her, the combination of his male heat and the heat of his sun-warmed clothes pleasantly scorched her back from her shoulders down. Caitlin's hands automatically lifted to rest over the backs of his.

Reno's lips found the side of her neck and nibbled gently. "I need to go to San Antonio for a couple of days," he said against her skin, then pressed an open kiss there. His hands moved up from her waist and covered her breasts. Caitlin gripped his wrists, her legs suddenly too weak to stand. "Come with me."

The gruff invitation landed heavily on her confused emotions. As if he sensed something was wrong, Reno lifted his mouth from her neck and nestled his cheek against hers. "You're shaking, Caitlin. And I bet you're having second thoughts about last night—" his hands moved from her breasts and he wrapped his arms tightly around her "—and what it all means."

His perception was a tremendous relief, and she nodded. He made a low growling sound. "Then come to San Antonio with me." He turned his head and pressed his lips against her flushed cheek. "You've only been to my place a couple times. Besides which, something tells me I should keep an eye on you."

The words made her freeze. "Maybe a few days away from each other would be better."

"Better than what?" he challenged softly. "Better than facing what you feel and starting to trust me?"

Caitlin shook her head. "I know what I feel."

"But you can't trust me." It was a statement. She heard the hint of impatience behind the words.

"Nothing lasts." Her voice was a strangled whisper and she bit her lip in silent punishment for giving so much away.

Reno's arms tightened gently. "That's right, baby, nothing lasts. Nothing that isn't respected or taken care of or encouraged lasts."

He gave her a few moments for his words to sink in. When she said nothing, he changed the subject.

"If I leave you here for a couple days, will you promise to be here when I get back?"

He was asking a lot. She started to shake her head, but stopped. "I'm not sure."

"I need more than that, Caitlin. I don't plan to lose you, and I damned sure don't want you to disappear from my life." He eased away and turned her toward him. "Unless you don't feel anything for me."

The grim look he was giving her made it impossible for her to evade him. But she couldn't tell him she loved him. Not when he only "wanted" her. "I do...feel something for you," she admitted. Reno's eyes narrowed on her flushed face.

"But maybe not enough."

She could barely maintain eye contact with the intense gleam in his eyes. She felt as if he could read her every thought and had guessed her every secret. She shook her head. "It's not that."

"Isn't it?" His thumbs rubbed slow gentle circles on her upper arms. "I reckon I can't force you to stay. I meant it when I said I was giving everything to you. If I have to hire someone to run it for you because you don't want to be here, it'll have to come out of the profits."

His hands relaxed and fell away. He reached for

his Stetson and eased back a step. His expression was utterly blank, but his blue eyes burned with tightly repressed frustration.

"If you'll provide me with a mailing address, I'll let you know how the transfer comes out," he said, his voice flat and all business. "If you're not interested in the responsibility, everything can be liquidated."

Caitlin nodded. Reno's sudden distance caught her by surprise. The granite set of his features reminded her of when he'd hated her. She needed no more than seeing that to realize how quickly he'd given up on her. If what he felt for her had ever had a chance of becoming something special to him or of lasting, he wouldn't have been so easily turned away. He was too used to making the world bend to his will to suddenly back off.

Instead, it was proof of what she'd feared, that Reno's interest in her was too shallow and too temporary for her to risk her heart on.

Her quiet "Have a safe trip," was all she could manage.

Reno's gaze was steady on her face a few moments more before it slid down over her. "I need a few things from upstairs, then I'll go."

Caitlin made herself glance away as he reached for his Stetson. Reno took that opportunity to leave the kitchen for the back hall. She leaned weakly against the counter behind her and listened to his boot steps go down the hall then up the back stairs.

Later, he came down the front staircase and went

out the front door to where he'd left his car parked the night before.

Caitlin turned toward the sink and gripped the counter as longing and regret started their inevitable war.

Caitlin passed those next two days at the Broken B. She spent more and more time outdoors. She even resumed riding, though she rode much longer and at a swifter pace than her doctor had given her permission to do.

And she missed Reno. The memory of every moment she'd spent with him since she'd returned to Texas made a circuit through her mind. She weighed his every look, his every word to her, everything he'd done. She eventually came to the conclusion that Reno's good character was too ingrained and too strong for him to switch loyalty easily.

She'd always believed him to be a man just like her father—stern, remote and unattainable. Yet now she couldn't pinpoint many qualities the two men had in common. She couldn't imagine Reno Duvall mistreating a child, whether it was his own or not. And his manhood wasn't so fragile that he'd crave only sons or resent a child for being born a female.

And Reno was surprisingly perceptive. Her father had never been sensitive enough to the feelings of others to care, much less recognize them or figure them out. The two men didn't value the same things. Reno valued good morals and responsible behavior; her father had valued daring and a spit-in-your-eye flaunting of the rules he disagreed with.

Besides which Reno, once he was convinced that he was wrong about her, had enough good character to change his mind and show remorse. He'd changed his mind and changed his behavior. Something Jess Bodine could never have done for anyone, because he'd believed he was never wrong and that everyone else had to change to accommodate him.

The two days Reno meant to spend in San Antonio ended up being a full week, then more. He called her a few times to let her know about the delays—and probably to see if she was still at the Broken B—but their conversations were stilted and awkward. Caitlin was disheartened by them.

Meanwhile, Jess's lawyer had called the ranch for Reno, but Mary had directed him to call the Duvall Ranch. When Mary told her about the call, Caitlin figured the results of the blood test had come back. She was no more than mildly interested in how it had turned out.

Because Reno stayed away so long, Caitlin's cast came off and her headaches became only occasional. By the end of Reno's second week away from the Broken B, Caitlin's hope reached its lowest point.

CHAPTER TEN

CAITLIN was walking back to the ranch house one afternoon when she saw Madison St. John's black Cadillac pulling away from the house. Surprise and curiosity made her hurry to the back door. She found Mary in the living room, but her gaze went immediately to the huge flat package wrapped in brown paper that was leaning against the wall.

"Miss St. John's driver brought this by, Miss Bodine," Mary told her. "He said it was a portrait that Miss St. John found in the attic."

Caitlin walked directly to the covered frame. It could only be the portrait of her mother. She glanced toward the wide tall wall over the fireplace, and had a dim memory of long ago when a painting of her mother had hung there. The Civil War era swords that were now crossed over the space had been there since just after her mother's death.

Caitlin looked back toward the carefully wrapped frame and put out her hands to reverently touch the top of it. A sweet feeling of nostalgia tingled over her and she hooked a finger under the tapes that held the paper and pulled. Taking care with the task, Caitlin unwrapped the portrait, not allowing herself to look at the image until she dragged the last of the heavy paper away and stepped back.

"Why, it's you, Miss Caitlin." Mary's hushed exclamation echoed Caitlin's own first impression of the woman.

Against the backdrop of a field of bluebonnets and a stormy Texas sky, was a full-length pose of a proud, statuesque woman dressed in a white, long-sleeved blouse, ruffled at the V neckline and cuffs, with a blue-black divided riding skirt that ended midcalf over her black boots. The woman had straight sable hair that she wore long and loose. A few wayward strands appeared to dance in the artist's suggestion of a light breeze. She carried a black Stetson in one slim hand while she held a few stalks of vivid bluebonnets in the other.

She could have been a woman from any period of Texas history, and her beauty was breathtaking. Her hip-length hair was magnificent, but her face was lovely, with a sweet expression that Caitlin suddenly remembered with poignant clarity. Elaina Chandler Bodine's eyes were an electric blue, and her gaze was direct, yet oddly melancholy and wise beyond her years.

Caitlin stared into her mother's eyes and had the peculiar sensation that her mother was staring into hers. For the first time in fifteen years she was seeing her mother's likeness and it shocked her to realize how closely they resembled each other.

Memories of her mother surged back. Caitlin raised her hands to her lips and pressed hard, as if she could hold back the emotions she felt.

"Should we hang it, Miss Bodine?" Mary's soft-voiced interruption distracted her, and she nodded, but said, "Would you mind if I...have a few moments?"

Mary understood instantly and left her alone. Caitlin stepped back to a chair and shakily sat down, never taking her eyes from the portrait as she let this first long look take her back to her childhood and the bittersweet memories she had of her mother.

Caitlin and Mary hung Elaina Bodine's portrait in its old position of honor over the fireplace. The deep, moody colors of the oils lent a dramatic beauty to the room. Caitlin found herself drawn to the portrait, and that first day, she spent nearly all of her time in the living room, staring at her mother's image, remembering her.

Profoundly touched by her cousin's response to her request weeks ago for pictures of her mother, she gave Maddie a call the moment the portrait was hung. But Madison wasn't taking calls, so Caitlin left a message of thanks. She went to the den for paper and penned a more extensive thank-you, but was careful to keep it simple and straightforward. Madison couldn't have made it clearer that she wanted nothing personal to do with her, and Caitlin couldn't help the disappointment she felt.

Caitlin was drawn back to the living room and her mother's portrait. She was so emotional over its return that the unanswered questions about Elaina plagued her.

Had her mother been unfaithful to Jess? In lieu of the blood test results, the only way she could find out was to ask someone who might know. Lucky immediately came to mind. He'd been around all those years ago. He'd told her at the visitation that her father had no reason to doubt Elaina's fidelity, but how did he know? Perhaps he could tell her something.

She called the bunkhouse just after supper and invited Lucky to the main house. Lucky walked into the living room, hat in hand. His attention went instantly to Elaina's portrait, and Caitlin saw him abruptly go still. Neither of them spoke as the cowboy stared at the likeness. Caitlin tried to read the expression in the old man's eyes. Surprise, admiration, sadness...

"I remember when that was painted," he said at last, his gruff voice a bit choked. "Watched it done." He paused and seemed lost in the memory.

Caitlin was struck suddenly by the odd remark. Lucky was a cowboy, always busy with ranch work. When would he have taken time to watch a portrait painted?

As if he'd sensed the unasked question, he went on.

"Ol' Jess knew he'd married one of the most beautiful women in Texas."

When he went silent again, Caitlin asked softly, "Was she faithful to him?"

Lucky pulled his gaze from the portrait to look over at her. "A woman like her couldn't help the notice she attracted, but your daddy was crazy with jealousy over it. In his mind, she was too beautiful to trust."

"She didn't cheat on him?"

Lucky shook his head. "Never to my knowledge.

Besides which, she never had a chance to cheat on him, 'cause he had her watched.''

The news shocked her a little. "How do you mean?" She suddenly sensed something about her father that was even darker than the things she already knew about.

"Exactly how I said it, had her watched. She was never allowed to go anywhere without him, never allowed contact with any of the ranch hands, and no other men if he wasn't there with her. Couldn't even go out riding alone or drive herself to her mother's house in town without him havin' to go along. The times he couldn't watch her himself, he gave me the job.''

Lucky stopped and looked down at his hat, gripped the brim, then glanced up at the portrait. "Which was why I saw that picture painted. I was the only man Jess trusted to keep an eye on her, and the portrait-painter was a man.''

Caitlin tried to absorb the information. Lucky went on quietly. "A week or two before she was killed in the car wreck, Jess took it in his head that I couldn't be trusted neither.''

Confused by that, Caitlin shook her head. "But he kept you around, you've worked for him all these years..." And Jess had tolerated Lucky's defense of her. If he'd thought Lucky had betrayed his trust, why would Jess have allowed him to stay on, then put up with Lucky's interference?

Lucky nodded. "Yep, he kept me around." He turned quiet eyes on her. "But that was 'cause of you. Had the idea that you were mine. Crazy part was, he knew Miz Elaina was expecting with you before I come to work on the Broken B. Only Jess got to thinkin' that since I'd worked on the ranch her mother owned, we'd musta had somethin' goin' and I'd followed her here to keep on with it. Which couldn't of happened because I only ever saw Miz Elaina from a distance at the other ranch. Never even spoke to her, cause Miz Clara hardly ever brought her out from town. Could never get that through Jess's head.''

''He let you stay on the Broken B because of me?'' The answer to her question had come to her already, but she needed to hear it.

Lucky nodded solemnly. ''He was sure that you were mine. Thought he'd get back at me with the way he treated you. I almost left once, hopin' he'd let up on you, but he told me if I left the Broken B, wouldn't be nobody around to take up for you.'' He hesitated briefly. ''Even talked to a lawyer about getting someone official to step in, but since Jess never laid a hand on you, nothin' could be done that wouldn't have made him do worse.''

Caitlin stared at the old man. A large part of her heart suddenly wished that Lucky was her father, even though it would mean that her mother had been unfaithful. Lucky was by far the better man, honorable and kind and gentle, the complete opposite of Jess Bodine. The emotion that surged up was choking her. The old man nodded.

''I did what I could, though it warn't near enough to keep him from hurting you.''

The solemn look in the old man's eyes, the regret and affection, drew her. Caitlin crossed the room to him and hesitantly put her arms around him. She felt his discomfort with the gesture, but he put his arms around her and gave her a firm hug. His voice was oddly strained.

"Didn't do as good a job at it as needed to be done—"

"But you tried." Caitlin eased back and so did the old cowhand. "Thank you." He gave her shoulder an awkward pat, then dropped his hand.

"It gives me ease that things are workin' out for you now in spite of Jess, Miz Caitlin."

Caitlin held back the tears she knew would increase Lucky's discomfort. It was clear that he didn't know how to handle the strong emotions between them any more than she did.

Her soft "Yes, they seem to be," was a half truth that pricked her conscience. Things had worked out with Reno—to a point. But, other than sending the portrait, nothing had really changed with Madison.

The two of them lingered, and Lucky reminisced about Elaina. Later, he went back to the bunkhouse, leaving Caitlin alone to gaze at the portrait.

It was morning before she realized Reno hadn't phoned her the night before. That made it two days since she'd last heard from him and, when added to his two-week absence from the Broken B, she'd be foolish to think that anything would happen between them now. She would always be grateful that the attraction between them had gone no further than a few steamy kisses and restrained foreplay.

But then, she'd always feared Reno's attraction to her had a time limit. Her feelings for him were still as strong—and had grown stronger in his absence—but whatever he'd felt for her must have already waned. Hadn't she known it would? Hadn't she known that mysterious something about her that had jinxed her father's affection for her would also affect Reno?

After finding out the extent of what Lucky had tried to do for her, she felt less flawed, less unlovable. But she was still reacting to what he'd told her, and it had yet to fully impact the insecurities she'd had her whole life.

Lucky's revelations had explained a lot about her father's treatment of her, but it was a fact that there'd never been anything about her lovable enough to soften Jess's heart. It was also a fact that even if the blood test proved she was Jess's daughter, he'd wished her enough ill to deny her a full inheritance. And he'd bequeathed her something that would put her in close proximity of the man he believed hated her.

Caitlin struggled with the torment of it all. She would always love Reno, she would always want to be a part of his life. They truly would always have a tie to each other, that much she was certain of. There was too much history between them, and they'd shared too many life-changing events for their connection to each other to completely break.

That didn't mean that anything would ever come of the sexual chemistry between them. Reno had been gone too long for her to cling to any realistic hope in that area.

Somehow, she'd survive this. She'd survived every

other disappointment she'd ever had, and she'd find a way to survive this one, too.

Caitlin was still at the house that morning when Mary came into the den and announced that she had a visitor. Caitlin immediately pictured Madison and her spirits soared for those seconds before Mary told her the visitor was neighboring rancher, Lincoln Coryell.

Lincoln Coryell owned the massive LC Ranch to the west. Caitlin had only met him a couple of times when he'd bought her grandmother's ranch, but that had been years ago. He hadn't attended either her father's visitation or his funeral, but she recalled now that he hadn't particularly liked Jess Bodine. She'd heard that he'd made a fortune in land, cattle and oil, and that he'd bought up several smaller ranches near her grandmother's ranch and had combined them all into one huge holding.

He'd grown up poor and uneducated, but he'd had a strong work ethic and enough business savvy to make up for it. He was also one of the most eligible bachelors in that part of Texas. Why he would come to the Broken B to see her was a mystery.

He was gazing at the portrait of her mother when she walked into the living room. He heard her come in and turned.

Lincoln Coryell was a big man, as work-hardened and tough as any cowboy who'd worked outside all his life. His hair was longer than his collar, and without the cover of the brown Stetson he held in his big hands, his hair was a thick, glossy black. His dark eyes were nearly black as well, and his chiseled face was ruggedly handsome.

"Hello, Mr. Coryell," she said, a little uneasy with the intense way he studied her face. "Would you like to sit down? Mary will bring a coffee tray in a moment."

Linc nodded, then stepped over to the nearest wing chair. Caitlin took a spot on the sofa across from the chair he'd chosen. He sat down after she did.

"That portrait is a perfect likeness of you, Miz Bodine." His dark eyes wandered back to it briefly before they came back and fixed steadily on her face. "Though you're even more beautiful in person, if you don't mind me sayin' so."

The gallant remark startled her. "Thank you, but that's a portrait of my mother."

His gaze shot back to the painting as if he didn't quite believe her. After a few moments, he returned his attention to her. Mary carried in the coffee tray then, and poured them each a cup of coffee. Linc politely had a sip, but when Mary stepped out of the room, he got right to the point of his visit.

"I understand that Reno Duvall is transferring his half of the Broken B to you."

The straightforward statement caught her by surprise. She felt her face heat. "I haven't been officially notified that I qualify to inherit half of the Broken B." Since she didn't yet know the outcome of the blood test, she didn't know if she could inherit anything.

Linc's mouth was a no-nonsense line. "Reno told me he wasn't interested in any official inheritance.

The Broken B is yours to do with as you like once the legalities get straightened out. He seemed to think there was a possibility you might sell."

Caitlin was too stunned to speak for a moment. Linc's stern mouth relaxed into a faint curve.

"Pardon me, Miz Bodine. You look like all of this is a bolt out of the blue for you. I realize you probably haven't made up your mind about anything yet, but I wanted to stop by. If you do decide you want to sell out, I'd like to be the first to make you an offer."

Caitlin stared, a little overwhelmed. Lincoln Coryell's business reputation for predatory swiftness must have been earned. She wondered if his reputation for ruthlessness was as accurate.

Caitlin set her coffee aside. "I'm not sure what will be done about the Broken B. If I do have a part in any decision to sell, I don't have a problem with you being notified about it before other buyers are sought. Unless Mr. Duvall objects."

Linc's dark gaze held hers those next seconds as if he was weighing the sincerity of her words. The hint that he somehow mistrusted her made her think about Beau's death. He couldn't have lived near Coulter City all this time and not known about it—or had an opinion.

"You seem…skeptical about what I just said, Mr. Coryell." She needed to face this head-on. Reno seemed to think everyone had changed their minds when he'd changed his. It could be that Lincoln Coryell was one who hadn't.

"People resent me, Miz Bodine. They tend not to like upstarts who buy their failures and make money on 'em. Your father wouldn't let me on the place. Reno Duvall has a more neighborly attitude. I was tryin' to figure which way you were thinkin'.''

Caitlin was a little shocked by his bluntness, but his answer relieved her. ''My father and I saw eye-to-eye on almost nothing, Mr. Coryell.''

One side of his handsome mouth quirked in approval and he leaned forward to dig his wallet out of his back pocket. He opened it and pulled out a business card that he handed her across the coffee table.

Caitlin took it and glanced over the raised letters of his name before she lifted her gaze to his.

''Would you happen to know when Reno's comin' back to Coulter City?''

Linc's question made her uncomfortable. She had no idea when Reno was coming back—or if he was coming back. ''I haven't talked to him for a couple of days. I can let him know that you'd like to hear from him.''

''If he's in San Antone, I can give him a call later,'' he said, then stood up. Caitlin stood also.

''Thank you for the coffee, Miz Bodine. I'll look forward to seein' if you and I can do business.'' He held out his big hand and Caitlin automatically reached for it. The moment the brief handshake was done and he'd released her hand, he glanced toward her mother's portrait.

''Your mother was a beautiful woman, Miz Bodine.'' His warm gaze returned to hers. ''But her daughter is even more so.''

Caitlin wasn't comfortable with the praise, but she

made herself smile. "That's kind of you to say, Mr. Coryell."

"No kindness to it, just good eyesight." His dark eyes glittered down at her for a second or so, then he reached for the Stetson he'd set on a side table. The male interest in his gaze had shaken her, but she felt no glimmer of interest in return.

She walked with him to the front door, then closed it once he stepped out. She watched as he walked to his car and got in. Though she could see for herself that he was a handsome man and very appealing, she couldn't summon more than that almost clinical observation.

Reno Duvall was the only man who'd ever affected her that way. Perhaps he was the only man who ever would.

Caitlin drove into Coulter City that evening. Mary liked to take an extra evening off occasionally, and since she'd asked for this one, Caitlin had agreed. She did a little shopping and ate supper in town, but instead of going straight home, she went for a long drive. By the time she pulled into the ranch drive it was after ten o'clock.

She gathered her few purchases and carried them to the house, letting herself in the back door from the patio. She'd seen no sign of Reno's car in the drive, so he wasn't home yet. Mary must have gotten home all right, because there were lights on in the kitchen and at least one on in the living room. Caitlin turned off the kitchen lights and walked quietly through the house to the living room.

She stopped in the den to check the voice mail for any calls from Reno, but there were none. Disappointment dragged her spirits lower, and she went on to the living room. She'd just stepped through the doorway when she caught the subtle difference in the room. The only light came from a small lamp on an end table whose dimmer switch was set on low. As she started toward it, she glanced automatically toward her mother's portrait.

The sight of the tall cowboy standing in front of the fireplace looking up at her mother's portrait startled her. She came to an abrupt halt.

"Your mother was a beautiful woman, Caitlin," Reno said quietly. "Except for the fact that this was probably painted when she was only a little older than you are now, anyone looking at it would think it was you."

Reno's voice was a low rumble in the quiet room. "When Coryell told me he'd like to marry you to get his hands on the Broken B, I figured I'd been in San Antone too long."

"I didn't see your car." The idiotic comment was the only coherent thought in her stunned mind.

"I didn't mean for you to."

Reno turned toward her. His gaze moved over her face, then took a leisurely tour of the rest of her before it came back to her eyes and narrowed speculatively.

"The cane's gone, your cast is off, and from the sound of it, you don't have a limp. How're the headaches?"

Caitlin brought her shaking hands in front of her

to grip them together. It wasn't a normal gesture for her, but she was painfully shy with Reno suddenly.

"I've only been having them occasionally. I'm not as easily tired either."

"That's good."

The silence between them stretched, and Caitlin's nerves stretched with it.

"Coryell is interested in the Broken B."

Caitlin nodded and glanced away. "So he said."

"The decision to sell is yours to make, Caitlin," he said softly. "The test results came back." He waited until she was looking at him to add, "You're Jess Bodine's biological daughter."

The official news didn't surprise her after her talk with Lucky, but it was a letdown all the same. It confirmed that her father had punished her—and from the sound of it, her mother and Lucky—for something his jealous mind had conjured up.

"A positive test result means that I've inherited only half of the Broken B," she pointed out. "Any decision to sell is also yours to make."

Reno shook his head. "Everything Jess owned is yours. As I said, it all rightfully belongs to you, whether you want it or not. Stay and run it yourself, or go and I'll hire someone to take care of it for you." He paused when he saw she was about to object. "I don't want any part of Jess's estate. I've left my ranch too long as it is. This last trip home made that plain enough."

Of course, she realized suddenly. He wanted to go home. He was probably weary of the Broken B and everything it must represent to him. His brother and mother had died here. And perhaps he now regretted their romantic involvement and wanted to distance himself from her. He might no longer hold Beau's death against her, but he might not be able to help that she was a reminder of it.

And now he would tell her so. He'd tell her that not wanting the Broken B and Jess's estate also meant that he didn't want her.

Reno came toward her then and stopped less than a foot away. The excitement of being so close to him stormed over her and left her weak.

"When I left, you admitted you felt something for me," he said, his gaze intent on hers. "I was wondering if you'd decided what that was."

The words sent a little shock through her. If he'd had second thoughts about her, why would he want to know what she felt?

She saw his stern, handsome face more clearly in the lamplight, saw the smoldering gleam in his eyes. It was a look that should have encouraged her to confess what she felt. But her fear of rejection—her fear of someday losing Reno—was too strong.

He went on as if she hadn't hesitated. "I thought you were falling in love with me, that maybe you already had but were afraid of your feelings." He lifted his hand and caught a lock of hair beside her cheek. "Or afraid of me."

Reno's perception made her breath catch and he released the lock to comb his long fingers into the side of her hair. "But then I thought about everything, and I came to a few conclusions." He brought his other hand up to her opposite cheek to slide it into her hair as he eased a bit closer.

"Your daddy turned out to be a jealous, hateful SOB. The blood test proved he had no reason to doubt your mother, but even if you'd been someone else's little girl, he had no cause to treat you the way he did."

Caitlin's gaze fell from his to conceal her hurt. "And yet he accepted Beau right away," she said before her breath caught on a small sob. She bit her lip to hold it back.

His fingers tightened gently against her scalp to bring her gaze back to his. "That doesn't mean there was anything wrong with you. Just means he wasn't man enough to live with the fact that he couldn't sire a son."

He gave her a sad smile when he saw the tears that welled in her eyes. She tried to move away from him to hide them, but he dropped his hands and slid them around her waist to keep her from evading him.

"That's it, isn't it? You think there's something wrong with you, some reason Jess couldn't love you. He loved Beau who wasn't his, but he couldn't love you whether you were his child or not."

Reno pulled her gently against him. Caitlin couldn't help that her arms went around him or that she pressed her hot cheek against his warm chest. She was shaking so hard that she gritted her teeth briefly to keep them from chattering.

She managed to tell him what Lucky had said about her father's terrible jealousy, and that he'd given

Lucky the task of keeping watch on Elaina until he'd come to suspect Lucky, too. When she added that Jess had hinted to Lucky that he'd treated her badly to punish him, Reno swore softly.

"Jess was a twisted fool." His arms tightened. "Don't let what he did twist you up inside, too."

He lowered his head and pressed his lean jaw against the top of her head. "You're afraid of your feelings, Caitlin, and you're afraid of me. I can feel it…"

Caitlin made a restless move but his arms held her firmly. "Maybe you think there's some reason I can't love you either, or that my love for you won't last."

He was identifying her deepest fears, and it was as painful as it was a relief. She pressed even closer to him as she sensed that he truly did understand her, that she might truly be safe with him. Something inside her was desperate for those things, desperate to at last be wanted and loved by him.

"But if you think I can't love you or that my love won't last, you'd be wrong."

Reno's words were soft, but powerful. She clung to him as hope and love swirled higher and higher in her heart. He moved his hands to grip her upper arms. To her dismay, he gently pressed her away from him. Alarmed, she glanced up into his rugged face, but he gazed down at her with a tenderness that eased her fear.

"I want you to be looking at me when I tell you I love you, Caitlin Bodine. What I feel for you goes too deep now to ever die, it's not frail and it's not temporary. I love you. I couldn't stop now, even if I was crazy enough to want to." A half smile lifted one corner of his handsome mouth.

Joy swirled over her so suddenly and so strongly that she felt herself sway.

"I love you, Caitlin," he said, then went solemn again. "There's nothing unlovable about you, nothing in you that I could ever turn my back on, nothing that would ever make me walk away from you and what we have. Not as long as either of us is alive."

The gruff words sent her joy spinning so high that she was dizzy with it. Her soft "I love you," was so choked she could barely get the words out.

"Don't be afraid to trust me, baby, don't ever be afraid." In the next second, Reno's lips crashed down hungrily on hers. Caitlin was equal to the passionate onslaught. Everything she'd ever wanted, everything she could ever hope for was promised and fulfilled in that wild, deep kiss.

It was a long time before Reno's lips eased away and they both stood breathing raggedly, their arms locked tightly around each other. The safety and security—the love—Caitlin felt in Reno's hard, strong arms was worlds more than she'd ever hoped to have.

His low, rough "Marry me soon, baby," was an order she couldn't refuse, and Caitlin agreed instantly, "Whenever you say."

When Caitlin lifted her head to look up at Reno, she caught sight of her mother's face over his shoulder. Elaina's jewel-blue eyes seemed to be glowing in the soft light and there was a hint of a sweet smile on her lips. The melancholy Caitlin had seen before suddenly wasn't there. Though she knew right away that the wistful impression might be caused by the angle of the light and the lingering blur of her tears, it gave her peace.

Reno's arms tightened around her, reclaiming her attention. She watched as his dark head descended and his warm lips settled possessively on hers.

If you enjoyed what you just read,
then we've got an offer you can't resist!

Take 2 bestselling
love stories FREE!
Plus get a FREE surprise gift!

✦ *Harlequin Romance*®

We're proud to announce the "birth" of a brand-new series full of babies, bachelors and happy-ever-afters: ***Daddy Boom***. Meet gorgeous heroes who are about to discover that there's a first time for everything—even fatherhood!

We'll be bringing you one deliciously cute ***Daddy Boom*** title every other month in 1999. Books in this series are:

February 1999 **BRANNIGAN'S BABY**
Grace Green
April 1999 **DADDY AND DAUGHTERS**
Barbara McMahon
June 1999 **THE DADDY DILEMMA**
Kate Denton
August 1999 **OUTBACK WIFE AND MOTHER**
Barbara Hannay
October 1999 **THE TYCOON'S BABY**
Leigh Michaels
December 1999 **A HUSBAND FOR CHRISTMAS**
Emma Richmond

Who says bachelors and babies don't mix?

Available wherever Harlequin books are sold.

HARLEQUIN®
Makes any time special.™

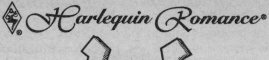

ℋarlequin Romance®

Coming Next Month

#3559 THE ONE-WEEK MARRIAGE Renee Roszel

Isabel has always played down her looks around her boss. But now he wants her to pretend to be his "wife" for a week, and she knows, as she sheds her drab feathers, Gabe will be in for the shock of his life!

#3560 TO TAME A BRIDE Susan Fox

Maddie St. John is everything Lincoln Coryell despises in a woman—she's glamorous, socially privileged and devotes all her time to looking good! Linc has to admit she's certainly gorgeous. But when they're stranded alone together, he discovers that Maddie isn't just a spoiled socialite. She has a loving heart—and Linc could be the man to tame her!

Rebel Brides: *Two rebellious cousins—and the men who tame them!*

#3561 FARELLI'S WIFE Lucy Gordon

When Franco Farelli had married Joanne's cousin, Joanne had graciously stepped aside, her love for Franco kept secret. Now he was begging her to stay, if only for his motherless son's sake. But Joanne needed to believe his desire for her wasn't because she resembled her cousin, but because he wanted her for herself....

Kids & Kisses: *Where kids and kisses go hand in hand!*

#3562 BACHELOR COWBOY Patricia Knoll

Luke had been an infuriating puzzle to Shannon since their first prickly meeting. Now he was desperate for her help, having been left in charge of his baby nephew. As she taught him how to take care of little Cody, Shannon saw that Luke's defenses were melting—just like her heart....

Marriage Ties: *The four Kelleher women, bound together by family and love.*

HARLEQUIN · FIVE DECADES OF ROMANCE · CELEBRATES

In July 1999 Harlequin Superromance®
brings you *The Lyon Legacy*—a
brand-new 3-in-1 book from popular
authors Peg Sutherland, Roz Denny Fox
& Ruth Jean Dale

3 stories for the price of 1!

Join us as we celebrate
Harlequin's 50th Anniversary!

Look for these other
Harlequin Superromance®
titles wherever books are sold July 1999:

A COP'S GOOD NAME (#846)
by Linda Markowiak
THE MAN FROM HIGH MOUNTAIN (#848)
by Kay David
HER OWN RANGER (#849)
by Anne Marie Duquette
SAFE HAVEN (#850)
by Evelyn A. Crowe
JESSIE'S FATHER (#851)
by C. J. Carmichael